SECOND GUESS

SECOND GUESS

Griffin Force #6

JULIE COULTER BELLON

OTHER BOOKS BY JULIE COULTER BELLON

Canadian Spies Series

Through Love's Trials

On the Edge

Time Will Tell

Doctors and Danger Series

All's Fair

Dangerous Connections

Ribbon of Darkness

Hostage Negotiation Series

All Fall Down (Hostage Negotiation #1)

Falling Slowly (Hostage Negotiation #1.5)

Ashes Ashes (Hostage Negotiation #2)

From the Ashes (Hostage Negotiation #2.5)

Pocket Full of Posies (Hostage Negotiation #3)

Forget Me Not (Hostage Negotiation #3.5)

Ring Around the Rosie (Hostage Negotiation #4)

Griffin Force Series

The Captive

The Captain

Cover Design by Steven Novak Illustrations

Copyright © 2024

ISBN-13: 978-1-7363129-9-5

Printed in the United States of America

First Printing March 2024

10 9 8 7 6 5 4 3 2 1

ACKNOWLEDGMENTS

I got extremely ill in September of 2021 and nearly died. It has been such a long road to recovery and there were times when I thought I would never write again. I'm so grateful to Becky, Jennifer, Michele, Jon, Jeni, and Robyn who cheered me on, read the book for me and helped me make it better, but most of all, they never let me give up and were always there for me. Thank you my friends, from the bottom of my heart! I am also so glad for a sprint group who motivated me when I didn't know if the words would come that day or any day.

I couldn't have done any of this without my loyal readers who emailed me and asked about the book and never let me think I was forgotten. Thank you to all of you!

And I really have to thank my husband and children. It's been a rough road, but we made it through together. I'm so glad I'm still here with the people I love and doing the things I love most with all of you. I love you!

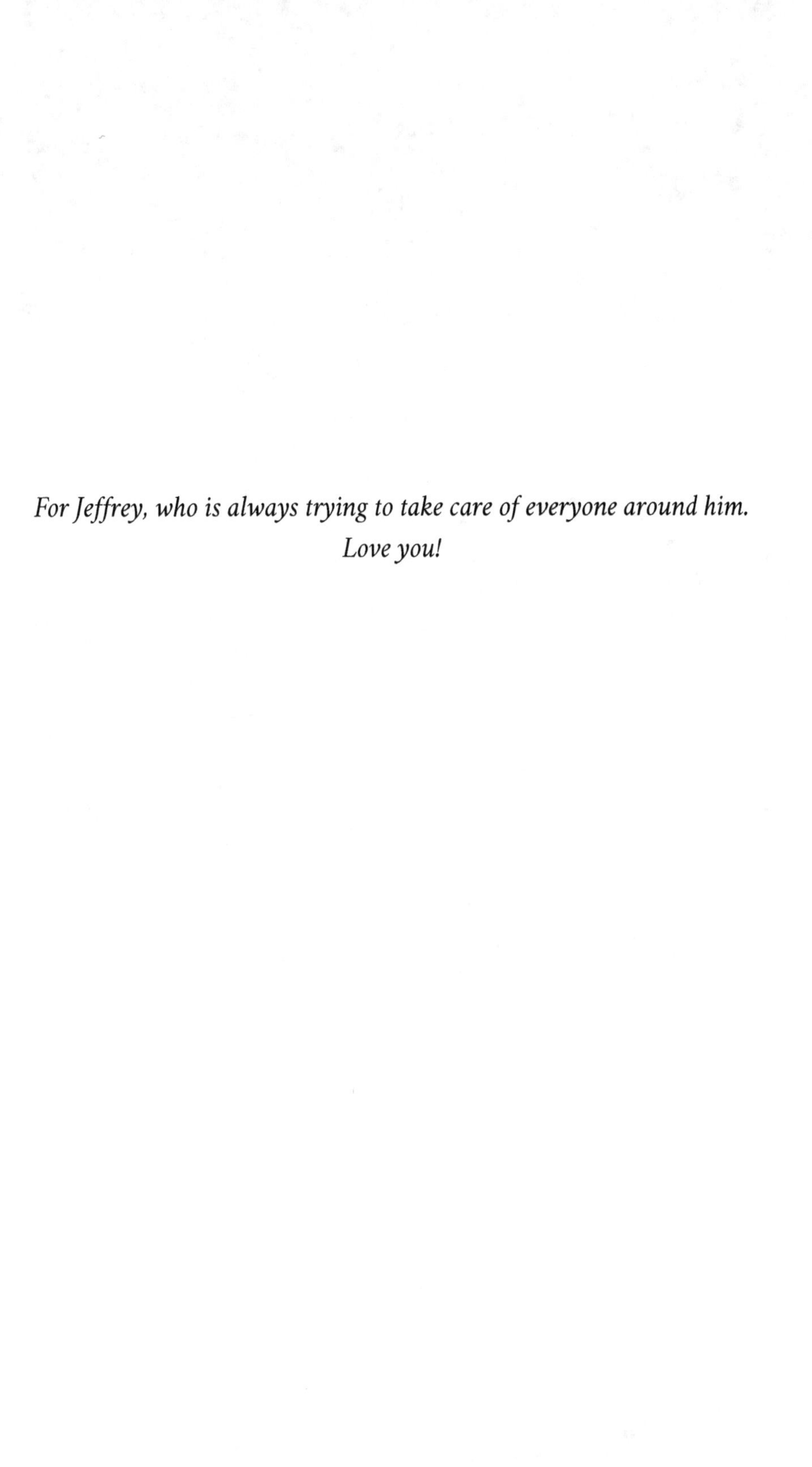

For Jeffrey, who is always trying to take care of everyone around him.
Love you!

CHAPTER ONE

Adrenaline pounded through Elliot's veins as he listened to Fahad screaming obscenities at the pilot who was silent in response to the terrorist's rant. There was no doubt in Elliot's mind what was coming. He closed his eyes when the gunshot rang out from the cockpit. Clenching his fist, he drew in a breath. There was nothing he could have done. He'd nearly blacked out after being pistol-whipped and it was all he could do to sit up straight. Pressing the compress tightly to his head wound with his other hand, he slowly leaned forward in his jump seat, his gaze on Atwah's gurney. He was still breathing, even after the complications of surgery, though his prognosis was unknown. How had Atwah's men known he was being transferred? Who had helped Fahad take over the plane? Elliot had so many questions and no answers.

The plane tilted slightly as the wings dipped, heading away

from the airfield where Griffin Force had been waiting to board. What a mess. He should have recognized Fahad or felt some sense of danger when he'd wheeled Atwah into the plane, but he hadn't. He'd felt safe. They were so close to finishing the mission and he'd let his guard down. Elliot pulled the compress away from the side of his head and winced at the pain. At least it had mostly stopped bleeding for now. He slowly turned his head from side to side, the dizziness seeming to have subsided. He wouldn't make the mistake of letting his guard down again. He lifted his gaze to Fahad. He'd seemed jittery and angry until the plane had finally leveled off and they were cruising at altitude. Ever since then, he'd been a bit more relaxed. Somehow that probably didn't bode well for Elliot. An unconcerned terrorist was sure of the plan in place and he definitely wasn't worried about being found or held accountable for his actions.

Fahad finished speaking to the man guarding the cockpit and started back toward Elliot. His mouth was once again pulled into an angry line and Elliot's stomach tightened. What now?

"Get up," Fahad commanded when he got close.

Elliot slowly stood, drawing himself up to his full height. He wadded up the bloody compress in his hand and waited for Fahad to speak.

Fahad glared at him, cold anger in his eyes. "If I didn't need you, I would kill you where you stand," he snarled. "But let me make myself clear: if Atwah dies, you will die next to him. Your only worth is in keeping him alive. Is that clear?" Fahad shoved him in the direction of Atwah's gurney. "Get over there."

Elliot caught himself on the wall and looked at Atwah's still form before he bent to check the monitors. They'd done the best they could to stop the internal bleeding in the operating room. All he could do now was make sure he kept breathing.

Fahad watched him for a moment, then turned away when his guard emerged from the cockpit, dragging the now-dead pilot. The guard pulled him to a spot near the front of the plane and left the body there, the pilot's face turned toward the wall. Elliot clenched his jaw. None of this should be happening. Griffin Force should be on this plane, escorting Atwah to a tribunal to be tried for his crimes. But instead, Elliot was tasked with saving the man who had hurt so many. He stared into Atwah's pale face. How would the world have been different if Atwah had been killed years ago? Would his death make a difference now?

"Is Muhammed in place?" Fahad asked the guard who was standing over the pilot's body. "Do we have everything we need to get to Amira?"

"Yes. All is as planned." The younger man dipped his head in deference.

Fahad glanced Elliot's way. He quickly looked down and adjusted Atwah's oxygen mask, but his mind was racing. Atwah had a daughter named Amira, though she was presumed dead. Was she alive?

Elliot heard a sniff from the other set of seats near the gurney. He'd almost forgotten about the Libyan nurse who'd accompanied them on the plane. Her wide brown eyes watched the men in the cabin as if she were the prey about to be pounced on.

"D-do you speak English?" Elliot asked her, keeping his

voice down. Even with all the stress of the plane being hijacked, his stutter had stayed manageable. He hoped he could keep it under control.

The nurse stood and moved closer to him. Her eyes were large as she looked between Atwah and Elliot before she answered. "Yes. Do . . . do you think he will kill me?"

"I'll do my best to make sure that doesn't happen," Elliot assured her. "Like he said, they need us right now, so until the plane l-lands at least, I think we're safe."

She grasped the edge of the gurney, her brow still furrowed with worry. "Where do you think they're taking us?"

"I d-don't know." Elliot looked out the small airplane window, but all he could see was blue sky and a few white, wispy clouds. "But my friends will be looking for us."

The entire team would be putting every resource toward finding them. He could imagine Colt mobilizing and handing out orders, putting calls in to their sources. Each team member had skills that would help in this situation, and that gave Elliot some comfort, though Fahad had obviously been planning this down to the last detail. How had they not seen or heard even a whisper of Atwah's planned escape? Had someone sold them out? That seemed the only explanation. But who?

The nurse leaned in, her face focused on the numbers flashing across the small screen behind Atwah's head. "The patient's pulse oxygen is low," she said quietly, darting a glance at Fahad, who was now standing near the cockpit.

Elliot looked at the monitor. She was right. He immediately turned up the amount of oxygen flowing into Atwah's mask. "Let's get those n-numbers up," he said to the nurse.

Fahad must have noticed the activity at Atwah's bedside. He strode over, pulling the gun in his hand closer to his chest. "What's going on?"

"Nothing out of the ordinary. He just needed a little extra oxygen," Elliot told him.

"You better not be lying to me." Fahad's fingers clenched the gun in his hand tight enough to make his knuckles white. He stared at the monitor, as if he were willing it to make sense to him. "There will be consequences. I'm to keep you alive, that doesn't mean you can't live with a little pain."

Elliot shook his head, doing his best to hide he was already in pain. "I'm not l-lying. Atwah is receiving the best care we can give him on an airplane. How long until we land and he can be transferred to a hospital?"

"Just do your job." Fahad looked at the nurse. "What is your name?"

She shrank back, as if hoping the wall would swallow her whole. "Nabila."

Fahad gave her a once-over. "You are under the same orders as the American. Keep Atwah alive, or you will die with him. And I'll be watching you."

Nabila nodded. "I will," she told him, her voice shaking. "I will do everything I can."

The alarms were starting to beep in earnest now as Atwah's oxygen level dipped even further. His heart rate was erratic and his blood pressure was dropping. Elliot quickly made sure the IV fluids were wide open and turned up the oxygen to the highest level. Nothing seemed to help.

Fahad moved in, his gun at his waist. "Do something!"

"Stand back!" Elliot barked. "If he dies, it will be your own f-fault for getting in our way!"

Nabila got on the other side of the gurney. "We're going to have to intubate." She grabbed an intubation tray, ripping off the protective cover. "Ready," she said, her voice full of authority now, as if the emergency had brought her confidence back.

Elliot looked down at the man who had murdered dozens of people and caused suffering for thousands. For a fleeting moment, the thought of not performing heroic measures to save his life went through Elliot's mind. But then he bent down and got to work. It was his duty to do all he could to save his patients. No matter who they were. He switched to high-flow oxygen. "Wait. Let's try this first."

They stared at the monitors. Intubation under these circumstances would complicate everything, so Elliot wanted to avoid it if he could. The airplane's cramped quarters weren't easy to work in and Fahad was still standing too close, but Elliot did the best he could with Nabila's help to adjust the high-flow oxygen and find what level would be enough to try to stabilize the patient. After the first few moments, their movements were in sync as if they'd cared for patients dozens of times together. She was a competent nurse, able to do what needed to be done and it didn't take long before Atwah's vitals started to normalize. The alarms stopped beeping.

Fahad stood over Atwah's unconscious body, watching them all closely, his gun at the ready. "You're lucky. Do not test me," he growled out.

"We'll do our job, you do yours," Elliot said with an edge of anger in his voice. "We don't need to be threatened while we w-work."

Fahad grunted, but backed off. With one final glare at Elliot, he returned to the cockpit area. Elliot sat down in a seat, his head throbbing. They needed to do more tests on Atwah, to see if he was still bleeding internally or if there was something they'd missed. But on a plane, they'd done all they could do. Elliot wiped at the thin trail of blood still trickling down the side of his face, frustration in the movement.

"You should let me stitch up your wound," Nabila said quietly.

"I will, once the bleeding has completely stopped and the swelling has gone down." He probably had a mild concussion and he'd been running on adrenaline for the last hour. It was starting to wear off and exhaustion crept over his frame. He pinched the bridge of his nose and let out a long breath. He needed to stay alert.

"Do you think they'd mind if I used the restroom?" Nabila asked, looking toward Fahad and his guard, her forehead creasing with concern.

"They'll want to keep us c-comfortable so we can treat Atwah. I think using the restroom would b-be okay," Elliot told her. At least he hoped so.

She nodded and moved toward the restroom door. The men barely acknowledged her, already deep in conversation. Once she was inside, Elliot held his head in his hands. He had to do something to alert Colt to their whereabouts, but what could he do? Fahad had already taken their phones. He glanced over at the body of the U.N. pilot that had been shot. Maybe he still had a phone. Did he dare try to get close enough to check?

He stood and headed for the body. Fahad and his guard didn't seem to notice him, and he knelt down as quickly as possible. Elliot quickly ran his hands over the pilot's clothing and felt the outline of a cell phone in the man's right pants pocket. He pulled it out and turned it on. Lifting the pilot's hand, he used his thumb for the biometric ID and the text screen popped up. There was an unfinished text to his supervisor.

"What are you doing?" Fahad demanded, his voice close behind him. "Get back to Atwah."

"My job is to help all that are w-wounded." Elliot quickly pocketed the cell phone, sending up a prayer the screen would stay on until he could send a text of his own. He wouldn't have another chance like this.

"That man is dead. You can't help him now." Fahad loomed over Elliot where he crouched on the floor.

"You d-didn't have to kill him," Elliot said, looking down at the pilot. The man was older, probably in his fifties. Working for the U.N. had undoubtedly seemed like a safe enough government job and he'd been doing a favor for Rian's dad. Elliot's heart squeezed, and he wished again that he could have done something to save him. "Can we notify the man's family?"

"No." Fahad jerked him to his feet and Elliot felt the heaviness of the phone in his pocket. The pilot might not have survived, but his phone could be the one link that could save them.

Elliot held up his hands in surrender as he walked down the small aisle back to Atwah. Walking past those empty seats where his Griffin Force teammates should have been sitting was a reminder of how alone he was and how much he missed

Griffin Force having his back. If he could just get a text to them, they'd have a chance to thwart whatever Fahad had planned. Reaching Atwah's gurney, he stopped to make some adjustments to the monitors as Nabila appeared at his side.

"I heard them," she said breathlessly, looking over her shoulder.

"H-heard what?" Elliot asked, keeping his voice down and hoping she would do the same.

"We're going to Idlib. Syria." Her eyes were wide. "We're meeting Atwah's daughter there."

Elliot could hardly contain his surprise. Not that they were going to Syria---he'd suspected that---but were they really meeting Atwah's daughter? No one had seen her for years. She'd been sequestered away for so long, most in the intelligence community thought she'd been killed early on in the war on terror. "Are you sure?"

Nabila nodded.

That changed things. Idlib was lawless and the perfect place for a terrorist to hide and regroup. But how did Atwah's daughter fit into the picture?

He had to get word to Colt.

Glancing behind them, Elliot could see Fahad still talking to the guard near the door of the cockpit. This was probably the only window of time he'd get to try and contact someone. He moved to the side of the gurney and pulled out the phone, relieved when he turned it on that it wasn't asking for the fingerprint again. Nabila moved closer, to help shield his movements, and Elliot typed out one word to Colt. *Idlib*. A little bead of sweat rolled down his back, needing this text to go through.

"What's going on?" Fahad said, his boots thumping on the floor as he approached. "What are you doing?"

"We're c-consulting on our patient," Elliot said, half-turning toward Atwah, frantically trying to press send. "Making sure his oxygen stays stable. Nothing more." He slipped the phone onto the gurney and covered it with a corner of the sheet, hoping Fahad would just think he was adjusting it over Atwah. He couldn't tell if the text had gone through or not, but he hoped with everything in him that it had. It was his only chance for rescue at this point.

Fahad's eyes narrowed. "Sit down. Both of you."

Nabila turned to do what she was told and Elliot followed her to the jump seats. Fahad stood over them, waving his gun near their faces as he yelled more threats, rehashing all the things he'd already said, as if he was set on repeat and had no other setting.

And then the unmistakable ring of a phone came from the gurney.

Elliot's heart sank. This could not be happening.

Fahad's head whipped around and he quickly moved to the gurney and snatched the sheet back. He held up the phone. "This is what you were trying to hide?" He dropped it to the ground and smashed it with his boot. "Who does the phone belong to? Which one of you was using it? Were you trying to call someone?"

Neither answered. Fahad grabbed Nabila's hair and yanked it, tilting her face up to meet his. "Was it you?"

Elliot stood and tried to put himself between Fahad and Nabila. "It was m-me, okay? Leave her alone."

Fahad let her go, but put the muzzle of his gun to Elliot's

chest and pushed in. "If I didn't have orders to keep you alive, you would be dead now." He curled his lip and sneered at Nabila. "Both of you."

"We've kept our end of the agreement. Atwah is still alive." Elliot kept his voice calm and even. Fahad was too unpredictable to antagonize.

Fahad's eyes flicked to Atwah, then back to Nabila, his eyes roving over her face and down her body. A slow, evil grin crossed his face. "We only need one of you to care for Atwah." He pointed to Nabila. "Maybe you should come with me and my men. We'd like to get to know our prisoner better."

His leer was unmistakable and from the look of horror on her face, Nabila grasped right away what his intentions were. She immediately shook her head. "No, I'm needed here. To help with the patient."

The air in the plane seemed to close in around them and Elliot's stomach twisted, knowing what Fahad and his guards could do if they got Nabila alone. He wouldn't let that happen. "I n-need her help to keep Atwah alive. I c-can't do it alone. His vitals have already crashed in the last half hour." He stood very still. "I *need* her," he repeated.

Fahad kept his eyes on Nabila, a smirk curling his lips. "No. You'll do exactly as I say." He grabbed her arm and pulled her to her feet. Nabila screamed and tried to jerk away. Elliot reached for the gun, wrenching it out of Fahad's hands. It skittered across the floor. Nabila was still struggling to get away, but Fahad's grip on her arm was iron-clad.

"Let her go!" Elliot yelled, throwing a punch that caught Fahad on the jaw.

He went down hard, taking Nabila with him. The gun was

on the floor just above his head and Fahad grabbed it. He pointed it downward, but Nabila caught hold of it as well. They struggled with it between them, each fighting for control. Elliot lunged forward, trying to get the gun and pull Nabila away from Fahad.

And then the shot rang out.

CHAPTER TWO

Eden stretched her neck and slowly rotated her ankle. Standing for hours in the shadows of a doorway, trying to remain as still as possible had made her foot go to sleep. She couldn't walk off the tingling numbness, as she needed to stay hidden, so all she could do was try to move into different positions to wake up her foot. Carefully straightening, she stared across the street at the only building on the block that still had a door. The former office building was nearly surrounded on all sides by burned and bombed out businesses. The rubble was mixed with garbage now, graffiti painted on the side of most buildings. Idlib, Syria, had been at war for too many years, and it showed. But this one corner building had been spared.

Two guards moved back and forth in front of the two-story building at regular intervals. They clustered around a barrel fire at times, but both of them were silent. Watchful. They weren't trying to hide their presence and no one approached them. The

AK-47s at their side probably made them feel invincible, but in Idlib, almost everyone carried a firearm of some sort. The AKs were practically commonplace.

"Anything yet?"

David's voice in her earpiece was whisper-soft, but still seemed loud to Eden in the early morning silence. "No," she said, keeping her voice just as low.

"I knew the American intelligence was bad."

"You just don't like our new source." Eden allowed herself a smile. David hadn't liked Luke from the start and didn't even try to hide his disdain for their new CIA friend.

"Former CIA guys are all the same. They think they have all the answers." David was on the opposite side of the building, watching, just as she was, but the earpiece made him seem much closer.

"Then it's a good thing Isaac sent us to verify the information." Isaac was a legend in the intelligence community, a former chief of Mossad, and head of Chol, the organization he'd founded after he'd had enough of being under a governmental thumb. She'd been honored to join Chol and trusted Isaac to do whatever it took to make sure they were acting on good intel. Eden rotated her ankle again. When she'd first joined, her only thought was to get out in the field to capture Atwah and put him in a prison where he couldn't hurt anyone anymore. He'd been more elusive than anyone had thought, but she'd worked her way through helping to capture smaller terrorists, inching closer to the one she wanted. Field work wasn't exactly what she'd imagined, though. Nothing happened quickly. The work was mostly boring---waiting for intel, waiting for a sighting, or word of a meeting. Lots and lots of waiting. Eden had worked hard on her patience levels. No matter what, though, she was grateful for the chance to be out here, doing her part to shut down any terrorist activity.

David's voice broke into her thoughts. "This is a wild goose chase. Our intel says Kabir is trying to offload four mid-range missiles. That's what we should be following up on, not watching for Atwah's daughter. Women have no value to him. If Atwah is looking for a safe haven, he'd go to one of his sons, not his daughter."

David's tone held conviction, and Eden thought he might be right. Kabir was newer to the arms dealing scene, but the intel on him was extremely concerning. If the information Luke had given them was good, though, and Atwah was on his way to his daughter, they'd have a chance to grab him. That was a huge opportunity they couldn't miss, and one Eden had been waiting for. But David had a point, there was no indication that Atwah had had any contact with his daughter in years. Why would he come to her, when he had several sons who could help him?

"We'll wait another half hour, then report in." Eden knew David wouldn't like the extra time added on, but she had a hunch they needed to wait a little longer. His annoyed grunt in her ear confirmed her suspicions, but he didn't contradict her.

She leaned against the wall again. Her feet were beginning to hurt after standing for so many hours. She was ready to sit down and have something to eat. David probably was, too. "I'll even buy you a bagel on our way to the office."

Maybe that would help him feel better about it. There weren't many places to buy a bagel around here anymore, but she'd found one corner shop that sold them, and she'd stolen away to buy one a few more times than she probably ought to when she was on ops. Eden told herself she loved the bagels and she was helping the shopkeeper so it was a win/win, especially since food, jobs, and money were scarce in Idlib. Besides, Isaac hadn't said anything about not going there again after she'd brought him a few. He was stuck in their command post nearly 24/7, so he'd appreciated the fresh food. Anything was better than an MRE or whatever they could scrounge up from the tiny refrigerator in the command post's kitchen.

She rolled her neck, trying to loosen her tight muscles. Sitting in the command post didn't sound so bad right about now. Actually, sitting anywhere sounded great. Just a half an hour more and they could head back to their makeshift operations center. It was on the other side of Idlib in a nondescript building that had once been full of apartments. It wasn't ideal, but suited their needs for this job.

Eden glanced at her watch. Maybe a half an hour was too generous. Maybe she should just call it a wash and head back to the office. They'd monitored the area for hours and had nothing to report. Just guards who seemed to be guarding an empty building. She looked at the men again, their bored faces the same as when they'd come on their shift four hours ago. Heavy gray clouds hovered above them, adding another layer of dinginess to the already drab landscape. It was as if the sun wasn't allowed to shine here anymore. If the light wasn't obscured by the shadows of the clouds, it was blocked by the smoke of war rising from the ground. Though no bombs or fighting had been reported in Idlib for a month or two, the charred smell of burning buildings and belongings still seeped from the ground to the air.

With that dismal thought, she decided to go ahead and tell

David to meet her at the rally point. But before she could speak, a van drove slowly down the street. That alone wouldn't have seemed odd necessarily, but a small sedan trailed right behind it. Two vehicles like that, in this part of town, looked suspicious.

"We've got movement," Eden said softly. "They're about to pass right in front of me."

"I see them," David said, his voice barely more than a whisper.

Eden held her breath as the cars passed. All the windows were tinted in the van, but she could see the driver's face. He didn't look familiar.

The van stopped in front of the building, and two guards rushed to open the doors. Eden slowly held up her mini-binoculars to see if she could get a look. The guards were pulling a gurney out of the back. Trying to focus in on the patient, she audibly gasped when she saw his face.

"It's Atwah," she breathed. "He's here."

But he wasn't looking good. His face was as white as the sheet that covered him. Before she could focus on any other details, her view was blocked when another man exited the van. He was tall, broad-shouldered, and his hair was military-short.

She strained to hear what they were saying, even though she was too far away. All she could hear was the murmur of voices. "What have you got, D?"

"That's definitely Atwah. I can see the scar on his hand."

Eden's heart hammered in her chest. She'd waited years to be this close to Atwah. She'd trained to be the best in her field in marksmanship and hand-to-hand combat, knowing she'd need those skills if she were ever to confront him. And in her heart, she'd sworn that if she ever had the chance to kill Atwah, she wouldn't hesitate. Now he was right in front of her, not more than 500 feet away.

But she couldn't do anything. Not yet.

The tall man walked beside the gurney, but his eyes were doing a methodical sweep of the area, stopping every few seconds to focus and observe. With his haircut, bearing, and a deliberate visual sweep, he must be military trained. Was he one of Atwah's people? Someone else Atwah had lured to his cause?

The guard pushing the gurney stopped in front of the building's door while the other guard opened it. A woman stood there in the doorway, as if she'd been waiting. Eden quickly put her binoculars to her eyes and goosebumps rose on her arms. If the pictures they had were accurate, Eden was looking at Atwah's elusive daughter, Amira.

Which meant Luke's intel was good.

Amira was dressed in black pants, a black blouse, and her dark hair was covered by a black and white hijab. As she looked down at her father, her face didn't show any surprise or sorrow. She merely moved back and let them in.

The guards quickly pushed the gurney inside, but the taller man hesitated. He looked around, his gaze coming to a stop right at the doorway of Eden's hiding place. Had he seen her? She froze. No, he couldn't have.

The driver gave the tall man a shove in the back and they all went inside and shut the door. Lights began to come on throughout the building. Their master had arrived. But Atwah wasn't looking as if he were here to put together another attack. From his pallor, it looked as if he'd come here to die.

Eden wouldn't mind if he did. That would make her job much easier.

"I guess the American was right after all," she said, keeping to the corners and shadows as she slowly made her way to David's position. "Amira was here and Atwah has joined her."

"Probably a lucky guess by some CIA source who's spent their life in front of a computer hidden away in a basement somewhere," David grumbled.

"Someday you're going to tell me what you have against former CIA officers," Eden said.

David's breaths were short and quick in her earpiece, which meant he was probably walking fast to meet her. "As soon as you tell me why you needed to take a leave of absence two weeks ago."

Well, she wasn't about to confide that in him or anyone. Her reasons for going to the U.S. embassy in Jordan was something she'd keep to herself. "I guess we'll both keep our secrets. For now."

"Are you at the car?" he asked

She slipped into the driver's seat and started it up. "Yes. I'm on my way to get you."

Carefully pulling into the roadway, she drove past what must have been a park at one time. The Hayat Tarir al-Sham group who opposed the Syrian regime had formed a rebel government of sorts and done its best to provide some structure in Idlib, but the ravages from years of war were on every side. Grass was torn up with a gaping hole in the middle, but a bench was on the side, untouched by any violence. As if it were waiting for normalcy, as if there would come a day when someone could sit down and enjoy the fresh air and a bit of sun.

That day wouldn't be coming anytime soon.

Atwah was in Idlib with his daughter. Now that her team had verified the intel, they could move forward with a plan. They could capture Atwah and see him punished for his crimes. And if that didn't happen, Eden would make her own plan.

She pulled over to the side of the road and idled for a moment as David got in the back seat. He kept his head down as she accelerated again, heading to the outskirts of town and home base.

"Could you hear what they were saying?" Eden asked, looking at David in the rearview mirror.

"The man beside the gurney was his doctor. Sounded American to me. Do you think the doctor is Luke's source? Maybe this is some sort of test to see what we would do if they shared information. It could be a trap of some sort." He looked out the side window. "I wouldn't put it past them."

"I don't think it's a test. Luke wanted the intel verified. He wouldn't have come to us for that if he had a man on the inside. He needed us." But if the man they'd seen was American, what was he doing at Atwah's side? He never let recruits that close to him, especially foreign ones.

"Well, Isaac has some hard decisions to make. I say we go ahead with our own plan to capture Atwah and leave the Americans out of it. We don't need them." David let out a huff of air.

This really wasn't like him. David followed orders, didn't question his superiors, and was one of the bravest men she knew. "What's going on?" she asked him softly.

He folded his arms. "Nothing I want to talk about."

"Fine." She couldn't force him to confide in her. "If you want my opinion, I think Isaac will ask Luke for any other intel he has, and we'll partner with him in capturing Atwah. He's got contacts we don't and access to CIA sources. His connections could help us get the job done once and for all."

And that's all she cared about. Making sure Atwah could never hurt anyone again.

"Do you think Isaac will issue a kill order?" David cleared his throat. "Because if he does, that means killing him will be your assignment."

Eden nodded. "He might." Part of her wanted that assignment---to take down the man that had stolen everyone she loved and the life she'd been meant to live. A smaller part of her worried that all the anger she'd bottled up for so long would cause her to make a mistake. To take away her chance for justice.

No, she had to bury her feelings deep. Whether her assignment was to kill or capture Atwah, she was ready. She had to be.

There was no turning back now.

CHAPTER THREE

Elliot rubbed his bloodstained hand on his leg, the last moments of Nabila's life playing over and over in his head. He'd done everything he could, but the gunshot wound had been too severe. Fahad had stood over Elliot as he worked to save her and walked away without a word when she was dead. She wasn't the first death Elliot had seen in this war, but seeing Nabila's lifeless body stabbed at his soul. He did his best to compartmentalize his feelings of rage and helplessness, but it was getting harder and harder to do that.

Focusing on the here and now and the task in front of him, he ducked down to avoid hitting his head on the ceiling as he pushed Atwah's gurney through the darkened tunnel. Fahad held the dimly lit flashlight in front of them with one hand and the other pulled the metal bar just below the thin mattress that Atwah was lying on. The stone and concrete floor was uneven, making it more difficult to maneuver the small wheels of the gurney while balancing his portable oxygen. Luckily, Atwah was strapped in tight. He still wasn't conscious, which worried Elliot. If he were, though, Atwah would likely be screaming in pain at the jerky movements. His unconscious state brought only silence beyond the sound of metal wheels bouncing over rocks.

Elliot squinted, trying to catch a better look at the woman leading them. Amira. She was Atwah's oldest daughter from his first wife. With as long as he'd been hunting Atwah, Elliot had read every bit of intelligence on the man. Not much was known about his daughters, but Elliot had seen the name Amira in a very thin file. She'd been isolated early in her childhood and mostly hidden for her entire life. There had been one small notation in her file when she'd married one of Atwah's advisors, but other than that, no one had seen or heard of her for several years. The one confirmed picture they had of her was from when she was younger. Seeing her now, she was taller than he'd imagined. Today she was wearing black pants and a black shirt, with her father's signature black and white checkered design on her hijab. She walked confidently, as if she was familiar with the uneven tunnel. Had she been living here? Is that why no one had seen or heard from her?

The tunnel seemed endless, but after walking what had to be at least another half mile, their little group turned down a branch that opened into a large room. Each corner held empty hospital beds with soundless monitors stationed beside them, as if they were waiting for patients to come. The room was illuminated with green-hued fluorescent lights that gave everything an other-worldly glow.

Amira adjusted her hijab before she gestured toward the far corner. Fahad pulled on the gurney, and Elliot had to quicken his step to keep up. After putting the gurney as close as he could to the waiting hospital bed, Elliot and Fahad transferred Atwah over to it, and Elliot quickly hung up the IV bag. A heart and blood pressure monitor were also available and Elliot set about hooking his patient up to it. When he was done and the monitor registered Atwah's heart rate, Elliot took a breath. The familiar beeping calmed him somewhat, though the numbers they showed weren't great. Atwah's blood pressure was low and his heart rate was high.

Amira approached him with a guarded look in her eye. "You are the doctor." It was a statement, not a question. Her dark gaze looked him over, measuring him. What he wouldn't give to know her thoughts.

He took a breath before he answered to hopefully control his stutter. "Yes. I'm Dr. Elliot Burke." He stood straighter and met her stare. Shadows played across her face, and for a moment he could see her father's features. The proud chin, the dark and fathomless eyes that seemed to look into your soul, seeing your secrets laid bare. Amira had a cold stare, but there was still life in her. Her father was known for the deadness in his gaze, a flatness to his eyes that gave even seasoned soldiers a shiver down their back.

"You've been brought here to keep my father alive." Her voice was imperious and commanding.

Atwah rarely let women into his inner circle, and the ones he did were usually soft-spoken servants. The intel the world agencies had on file seemed to think that Atwah's daughters were the same. Subservient. Quiet. But the woman in front of Elliot was confident and sure of herself, able to articulate commands without a qualm. What else had their intelligence sources been wrong about?

"Can you do that?" she asked, walking to one side and giving him a once-over as if she were a general inspecting a soldier.

Elliot flexed his hands. "I can try. There are no guarantees." He looked at her, a challenge in his eye. "Your father is gravely ill. He needs tests run to find out why he still hasn't regained consciousness, and beyond that, his survival might depend on his w-will to live."

"Then he will be just fine." Amira motioned toward the guard standing behind her. "Restrain him." The guard nodded and lifted a chain from the floor.

Elliot frowned and stepped back. "Hey, there's no n-need for r-restraints." His stutter was becoming more pronounced so he inhaled and held his breath for three seconds before letting it out. He had to stay calm.

Amira put her hands behind her back as the guard bent and slipped the chain around Elliot's ankle before he locked it into place. "I find that restraints prevent many problems," she said. "With no avenue of escape, you will concentrate on what you were brought here to do."

"What if my patient n-needs something that I can't get because I'm chained up?" He shuffled forward, dragging the chain along with him. It was iron and wouldn't be easy to get out of. But he'd have to try.

"That's not a concern. One of my men will be with you and get you anything you need." Amira watched him carefully. "You are American Special Forces?"

"I'm a doctor," he said firmly. She probably knew exactly who he was. It would be foolhardy if she didn't, and the

Atwah family was anything but that. Though, even with that background on her family, she might not be aware of his full identity quite yet, so he didn't plan on giving her any information.

"Yet you hunt my father." Her eyes were shrewd, as she waited for his answer. Was she testing him?

"No, I'm trying to keep him alive. Then maybe once he's on his w-way to recovery we can discuss how I can get home." The chain around Elliot's leg was heavy and his gut felt wrapped up in the iron as well. Being underground would make it nearly impossible for Griffin Force to find his location. The chances of him going home were getting slimmer by the hour the longer he was here and out of sight. But maybe he could bargain with them. "Surely in exchange for your father's life, I should b-be allowed to go home."

Amira touched the edge of the hijab that concealed her neck and cocked her head to the side as if considering his words. "We shall see if you can keep him alive first. There's no point in discussing something that may or may not happen."

"If I'm to keep your f-father alive, I'll need supplies." He looked around the room. "Monitors are great, but he may need specialized care."

Amira waved her hand. "Fahad will get you whatever you need. This is a fully stocked hospital."

"We're in an underground tunnel with b-barely any light- ing." There were boxes strewn about the edges of the room and the lights flickered on and off occasionally. Elliot couldn't even call this a field hospital, and he'd seen a lot of those. "This is a far cry from a fully stocked hospital."

"We're well-protected," she corrected. "And this *is* a hospital.

My father will have the best care. Due to the circumstances---for now---that is you."

Her tone had a finality to it. *For now.* He wasn't expected to be around long-term. Elliot had expected that, but somehow hearing it was a kick to the gut. "You know, if you have someone here that could help me, I'm happy to w-work with another doctor or nurse. In fact, that might be better in case something goes wrong. Having two sets of hands could become necessary." He swallowed, remembering what had happened to Nabila, the last person to help him with Atwah's care. He hated to put anyone else in harm's way, but in order to stay alive and make sure Nabila's death wasn't in vain, he'd probably need help keeping Atwah breathing.

"You are so anxious for my father's welfare." She raised her eyebrows. "It surprises and pleases me. But do not worry, I have made arrangements for you to have a nurse." She glanced at Fahad with a slight frown on her face. Had she heard about Nabila's murder? Did that upset her plan? Fahad didn't react to her frown, so it obviously wasn't pricking his conscience.

Her death weighed on Elliot, but he had to bury those feelings. Right now, he had to focus on keeping Atwah alive and figure out a way to escape and help Colt find him. Hopefully that text had gone through and Griffin Force was on their way to Idlib. Even if he was, though, the chances of Colt finding an underground hospital in Syria weren't great, so Elliot was going to have to send up a signal of some sort. He just needed time to think of exactly how to do that.

Atwah let out a small moan, his head moving from side to side. Amira turned and went to her father's bedside. She took his hand and lifted it to her cheek, then bent and spoke softly in his ear. His eyes fluttered, but didn't open. It was a tender scene and for just a moment, Elliot saw a daughter worried for her father instead of a woman protecting a terrorist who'd killed and hurt thousands of people. Elliot slowly shook his head, unable to turn away from the scene before him. He'd been awake for nearly twenty-four hours and had a splitting headache. He needed some sleep so he could stay sharp. Amira and anyone in the Atwah family exploited weaknesses and fed on fear. He had to be on alert at all times.

Glancing over at Elliot with a look of annoyance, Amira gently returned her father's hand to his chest. She closed her eyes for a moment, then squared her shoulders and straightened her spine. Opening her eyes, she motioned for Fahad to follow her to the far corner of the room. He did.

Elliot moved closer to the bed, his steps uneven, one foot held back by the chain noisily dragging behind him. Fahad and Amira looked over at him before putting their heads together. Fahad was speaking in a low, unemotional voice in Arabic. From what Elliot could tell, he was giving her a report of what had happened on the airstrip and on the way to Syria, repeatedly saying the mission had gone smoothly.

Atwah had lapsed back into unconsciousness. Elliot moved around to the other side of the bed, adjusting the IV, trying to watch Amira and Fahad without being obvious. They weren't paying him any attention. She was focused on Fahad, her arms folded, as if she didn't like what she was hearing. Her frown returned when he mentioned Nabila. She asked some questions and Fahad gave one-word answers. From the tense way he held his body, Fahad feared Amira, or at least her reactions to what had happened on the way here. Amira turned her back to Elliot, so he couldn't hear what she was saying to Fahad, but her tone was angry. Fahad bowed and apologized, but those words would never make up for Nabila's death.

Elliot stepped between the wall and the head of the bed, positioning himself a little closer so he could maybe hear more. He watched the heart monitor while his ears were attuned to the whispered conversation on the other side of the room. He only caught a few phrases here and there, but what he could understand chilled him to the bone. An arms dealer was coming to meet with them. If her father was still not available, Amira would stand in his place. They were buying something . . . and whoever was selling it wanted their money. Atwah had made a contingency plan that Amira needed to carry out.

Elliot groaned inwardly. In the last year Griffin Force had done everything in their power to thwart Atwah's plans of killing as many people as possible and forcing world governments to meet his demands. With his capture, Elliot had allowed himself to believe Atwah's reign of terror was over. That they'd finally won.

But they hadn't. Not if his daughter was set to step into his shoes and carry out his plans.

He stared at the man on the gurney, the one whose life he was trying to save while his plans to kill others were put in place. Exhaustion flowed over him. Colt would be looking for him, using every resource Griffin Force had. But would he think to look below ground?

"I need you to be psychic here, Colt." Elliot whispered. "Find m-me. Fast."

CHAPTER FOUR

Eden pulled her hijab closer around her face before she entered the tunnel. Isaac had tasked her to get as close as she could to Atwah---to see what his condition was and if the opportunity arose, to take him out. Adrenaline rushed through her veins as the darkness of the rock-hewn tunnel closed in around her. Quality medical care, especially for any condition that needed hospitalization, was hit or miss in Idlib, though the underground hospital was popular since it made people feel safe. The passageways hid an entire network of rooms that housed patients and doctors. It was large, and finding Atwah wasn't going to be easy.

She kept a steady pace, hoping she was headed in the right direction. A man approached her going the opposite way. Eden squared her shoulders. The best way to fit in was to look as if you belonged, so she kept her steps sure. He passed her with barely a glance. Voices were becoming more clear up ahead, and she licked her lips, going over her cover ID in her mind.

She was a nurse, sent to help the doctors in whatever way she could. It was common knowledge that the underground hospital was constantly understaffed. Hopefully no one would question her too closely, and they'd just be grateful for her skills.

Turning a corner, she entered a large bay area that was being used for triage. Several men were lying on the ground, one groaning in pain, holding his shredded pant leg. Through his fingers blood seeped from a large wound. Only one young man was on a gurney in the middle of the room, a doctor standing next to him, applying compresses.

"You there," a doctor called to her in Arabic. "We need an extra pair of hands."

Eden hurried to his side, quickly pulling disposable gloves out of her pocket and putting them on as she walked.

"Hold this compress while I get ready to cauterize the wound." The doctor turned to the nurse on the other side of him.

Eden concentrated on keeping pressure on the man's arm. His uniform was a mixture of two groups, his pants those usually worn by ISIS soldiers, his shirt from Hayat Tahrir al-Sham, a perfect representation of the confusion surrounding who was fighting who during this war. Regardless, both his shirt and pants were bloody, dirty, and torn, like so many others she'd seen. She glanced at his face, noting how young he looked. There had been too many faces just like his---young men who'd sacrificed their lives for a cause that they didn't necessarily understand, but were asked to fight anyway. She couldn't think too hard about any of that. If there was one thing this war on terror had taught her, it was that there wasn't a lot of justice in this world.

Eden watched while the doctor and everyone else surrounding the gurney fought to contain the blood loss and save the young soldier. It took some time but, in the end, they were able to stop the bleeding and stabilize the soldier. There was no way to tell whether he would live, but at least he had a fighting chance now.

The doctor stepped away and motioned for her to follow. "You did well. Are you new?"

She nodded. "Yes. I'm here to help." It was always best to keep to the truth as much as possible, and she did want to help. As much as she could, anyway, until her mission was complete.

"We are always in need of help." He swiped a hand over his brow. "Especially one with your level of calm in an emergency. Where did you receive your training?" He walked slowly, looking into small rooms, nodding to himself when he saw the monitors beeping steadily. It was as if he was doing informal rounds on a hospital floor, only it was a tunnel of rooms fifty feet underground.

"I trained at Damascus University," she said, keeping her voice soft. "My family was from eastern Ghouta, but I made them leave when the chemical attacks started. And then I came here." She held her breath, hoping the doctor wouldn't ask too many more questions.

"Ah, good for you for getting your family out." He stopped in front of a small room that was barely ten steps wide and turned to face her. "This patient needs some special care and I can't spare any of my other staff tonight. I'd like you to watch over him and monitor his vitals. He's scheduled for surgery as soon as I can get him in."

Eden was torn. The doctor had obviously accepted her enough to give her a job. But sitting with someone would prevent her from looking for Atwah. If she didn't accept, though, it might make her look suspicious. They had to believe she was a nurse there to help. "Of course."

She walked into the room and went to the patient's bedside. He was a child, probably no older than seven or eight. His small face stared up at her, his large brown eyes curious, but not afraid. "Hello," she said in Arabic. "What's your name?"

"Mahdi," he said softly.

The doctor joined her and smoothed back the hair on Mahdi's forehead. "This nice nurse is going to stay with you until it's time to go to sleep," he told the boy.

"And then my leg will be cut off," Mahdi said matter-of-factly. "And I will get a new leg."

"That's right." The doctor gave him a small smile. "And I will make sure you get a strong leg so you can still kick the ball across the field."

Mahdi smiled. "Thank you." He closed his eyes. "I wish my mama was here."

Eden swallowed and let the words wash over and through her, not allowing any to stick. She had to steel her emotions from feeling the sentiment. No matter how hard she tried, though, memories of her mother and father filtered through, then her brother. She clenched her teeth. No one had been with them when they'd died. When this endless war had taken their lives. Both her own mother and Mahdi's mother deserved to be with their children. The brutality of the war on terror had hit the women and children the hardest. But if Eden let every sad story affect her, she'd be sitting on the floor unable to do anything but cry. And then what good would she be? She couldn't think about any of it right now. She had to keep everything compartmentalized so she could focus.

"How did you hurt your leg?" she asked, sitting on the small stool next to the bed.

"A bomb hit our house, and we couldn't get out fast enough." He looked down at his right leg. "My leg was stuck under the big rocks for a long time. I couldn't help my family."

"His neighbor found him and brought him here." The doctor looked behind him at the monitors. "His blood pressure has been unstable and the surgeries are getting backed up. Three people are ahead of him and there's a limited amount of anesthesia. I'm hoping to have enough for him." His eyes were weary when he looked at her. "If you could keep an eye on his blood pressure until it's time for him to go in, my mind would be at ease."

Eden pressed her lips together, then nodded. "I'll stay with him." Tender feelings for Mahdi, and the life he was facing without a limb or parents to support him, were starting to overwhelm her. She took a breath and smiled at the little boy. "You're very brave."

He reached out his hand to her and she took it. "I'm glad you're here."

His sweet honesty surprised her and she squeezed his fingers. The doctor left, and Eden asked Mahdi if he had any brothers or sisters, if he had been to school, and what he liked to do the most in his free time. The boy quickly warmed to the topics, telling her that he didn't have a brother or sister, but did have a cousin he hadn't seen in a long time. He liked school and had learned to read, but his favorite thing to do was be outside with a ball. It seemed like they'd talked for hours, and Eden was enjoying herself. Mahdi was easy to be with, but all too soon another nurse was at the door and reality set in.

"We're ready." Her words were solemn, but she smiled at the boy.

Eden stood and let her fingers slide from Mahdi's. He gave her a little wave as the nurse maneuvered his gurney out of the room and down the hall. Eden put her hand to her mouth. This was why she'd joined Isaac's team. To do whatever she could to stop the war as quickly as possible and root out those who were using the chaos to make themselves powerful and rich. Men like Atwah who preyed on the weak and vulnerable for their own gain.

Stepping outside the room, she looked both ways down the hallway. There was some movement at the far end, but other than that, it was empty. Now was the perfect time to look for Atwah.

Walking down the hall, she glanced briefly into each room. Some were occupied, but most were empty. That was comforting in a way. There had been a few bombings lately, but perhaps not as many casualties as were first thought.

She turned down several hallways, then backtracked when they led to dead ends. After several tries, she finally found a tunnel which had several twists and turns and seemed slightly more hidden than the others. She followed it, her adrenaline ramping up again. If she was going to hide an international terrorist, this was the part of the maze that would be most likely.

The sight of a guard at the end of the tunnel seemed to validate her suspicions. He stood up from his wooden chair, the fluorescent light above him casting a green hue over his skin. "What are you doing here?" he growled in Arabic. When she didn't reply, he repeated himself again in French.

Eden walked steadily towards him and raised her chin. She was about to say she'd come to help when monitors inside the room he was guarding started beeping. The guard whirled and ran toward the sound. Eden followed.

The scene before her was one of controlled chaos. The doctor she'd seen accompanying Atwah into the house the day before was rushing to get the paddles ready to stabilize Atwah's irregular heart rhythm, but his movements were jerky due to a chain around his ankle. The monitor was beeping like crazy, the terrorist's heartrate fast enough to send him into sudden cardiac arrest. He needed an electrical reset.

Eden moved into the room. The guard looked stricken, his entire focus on the blaring monitor.

"Do something!" the guard shouted.

The doctor looked back at her. "Help me get the d-defibrillation pads on." His Arabic wasn't great, but it was understandable at least. He motioned with his head to some supplies on a small table near the bed.

Eden was frozen. This was what she'd wanted. Atwah's condition would likely lead to a cardiac arrest if they did nothing. If she helped the doctor now, then he might recover. But if she didn't, her cover was blown and the guard would shoot her on the spot.

"Nurse!" the doctor shouted.

Eden woodenly stepped toward the table and did as she was

told. Maybe it was too late. Maybe nothing they tried now would do any good.

Even dragging around a heavy chain, the doctor was a blur of motion as he worked to shock Atwah's heart into a regular rhythm. After the second defibrillation attempt was unsuccessful, he had Eden start CPR while he kept charging the paddles for the next round. What seemed like an eternity was probably only seconds as he murmured to himself the same words over and over. Eden listened closely to see what they were. "Come on, come on," he was saying. His accent was unmistakably American. How could he want to save the man who had killed his countrymen? Who had threatened and terrorized American citizens for so long? She wanted to ask. She wanted to shout to give up and let him die.

But then the monitor's alarms stuttered, slowed, and finally registered a strong, regular heartbeat again.

"Rhythm's b-back," the doctor said, wiping his brow. "We got it back."

Eden listened to Atwah's heart monitor steadily beeping and closed her eyes. He was back. But not for long, if she had anything to do with it.

CHAPTER FIVE

That had been close. Too close. Elliot sat on the wooden stool silently watching the monitors that said Atwah was still breathing and his heart was beating normally. The man had been within a hair's breadth of having a sudden cardiac arrest. Elliot knew it in his bones. But they'd managed to bring him back. Did Atwah have heart disease? A family history of heart problems? As a Griffin Force member, Elliot had never seen any intelligence reports indicating Atwah had health problems, but as his doctor that information would have been nice to know. With the injuries Atwah had sustained in Libya, he could have more internal bleeding, his brain might be swelling, there just wasn't any way to tell and Elliot couldn't order any tests to be run. He ran a hand through his hair. They'd have to watch him even closer now and do the best with what they had available.

The new nurse sat silently near the door, her head down. When he'd first seen her, she'd seemed familiar to him somehow, but he couldn't place her. He'd met a lot people as he'd traveled throughout the world on missions, but he did his best to not be memorable himself, to stay in the background as much as possible. She hadn't seemed to recognize him at all, but then again, they'd been in the middle of a medical emergency. There wasn't really time to ask personal questions.

He leaned back in his chair and waited a moment until he'd controlled his stammer. "Do you speak English?" he asked quietly in Arabic.

The woman slowly lifted her head. She had high cheekbones, full lips, and a slightly pointed chin. She tilted her head to look at him, her sable-dark eyes meeting his. "Yes." She folded her hands in her lap.

Elliot was relieved. His Arabic was passable, but not great. He switched to English. "What's your name?" She sat there unruffled, her calm demeanor showing through. He wanted to know more about her. She obviously had a medical background. And since Atwah was stable for the moment, they had time to talk.

"Eden. What's yours?" Her voice was accented, but he couldn't quite tell where she was from.

"Elliot Burke." He crossed one leg over the other and tried to get comfortable. "Are you from around here?"

"No. You are American." She tilted her head slightly. Was she expecting him to contradict her?

"Yes, I'm American." He watched her adjust her hijab and glimpsed her dark hair before she tucked a few strands more carefully inside the hijab once more. "How long have you been a nurse?"

She drew in a breath and a slight crease appeared in her

forehead, as if she was debating how to answer. "In a way, since I was a small girl. My father was a doctor and he often took me to assist him, especially when the war started."

Though she tried to hide it, there was a hint of wistfulness in her voice. She'd obviously loved her time with her father. "I thought you weren't from around here."

She pursed her lips. "There is war in many places."

Well, that was true. She obviously didn't want to talk about where she was from. "Tell me about your father." He kept his voice low and even, hoping she would feel like she could trust him.

Her eyes met his once more, her expression unreadable. She glanced into the hall, but then began to speak. "My father was a humble man. He only ever wanted to help people. He met my mother at the hospital. She was a nurse, and they worked together for many years. They never turned anyone away that came to them for help, even when it got dangerous during the war." She stopped talking and raised her chin.

"Did your father let you help him when it was dangerous?" He couldn't imagine a father putting his daughter in harm's way, but war required sacrifices that no one ever thought they'd have to make.

"There was no choice." Her body was completely still, as if she was trying to hold all her emotions in. Had that reaction been another consequence of war in her life? She looked at him, curiosity in her gaze. "What of your family? Why did you become a doctor?"

"For the same reason as your father. I wanted to h-help people." He let out a long breath. "War changed things for me, too. Caring for those who fight, and for those who are trying to survive the fighting, isn't anything like I thought it would be. I wish I could save everyone." He looked over at Atwah. "But there are those who c-can't be saved no matter what you do." Body or soul.

Her gaze followed his. "Do you think he will die?"

"I'm doing my best to make sure that doesn't happen, but he needs some specialized care that we can't get here." He rubbed his hand across the back of his neck. "If I can't keep him alive, they'll kill me." Elliot was surprised he could say it so calmly, but in a way, it didn't seem real, though he knew it was.

Eden's eyes widened. "If he dies, you die as well?"

"That's what I've been told. I'm really not a fan of their motivational techniques." He smiled, but she didn't return it.

"He's already near death. You're not a miracle worker." Her voice had an edge to it now, as if the news upset her.

"I didn't really ask for details. I've just been doing whatever I can to make sure he lives." Atwah's heart monitor beeped for several seconds in the silence between them, the sound a bit of comfort. As long as it was beeping, Elliot could let down his guard for a moment.

"You've got to get out of here." Eden glanced out into the hall again. "This man is in critical condition. He will die no matter what you do."

"Do you have such little faith in my doctoring abilities?" Elliot raised his eyebrows, one corner of his mouth lifting in a half-smile. "You've only seen me in action once and I *did* save him."

She didn't seem to appreciate his attempts to lighten the mood. "You could be the best doctor in the world and he'd still die. You cannot save him."

Eden stood quickly and walked to Atwah's bedside. She looked down into his face with such an intense expression he could feel the animosity rolling off of her. Eden was acquainted with Atwah somehow, and likely not in a pleasant way.

He stood, wincing at the chain rattle that followed him wherever he went, and moved to stand next to her. They both watched their patient. "He doesn't deserve to live," Eden whispered.

Elliot opened his mouth to respond, but there was a commotion at the doorway and Amira entered with her guards.

"Stand aside," she ordered.

Elliot and Eden took a step back and Amira took their place at her father's bedside. Snapping her fingers, she held her hand out, and one of her guards handed her an iPad with an app open on it. Lifting her father's thumb, she used his fingerprint to access what looked like a hidden file. Account information popped up on the screen, but before Elliot could see anything else, she tilted the screen away from him. Her eyes were glued to the tablet and after a long, few minutes, she looked at the man who stood in the doorway. "It's done."

"You need to leave. We have much to do," the man in the doorway said to Amira, his eyes never leaving her face.

She turned and scanned the room. Her gaze lingered on her father. "*Ma'a al-ssalamah,*" she murmured. With one last look, she turned to her guards, her command said in Arabic, but her meaning clear. "Kill them all and meet me at the entrance."

Elliot's blood ran cold. He looked from Amira to her guard. She was going to have her father killed.

And them.

Time slowed as Amira went through the doorway and the

guard reached for his gun. Seeing that movement spurred him into action. Elliot lunged for him, hoping his chain wouldn't hold him back. He managed to grab the weapon, but the guard didn't let go, holding on to the gun as if it was a lifeline.

"Run!" Elliot yelled to Eden. But the second guard was already moving toward her and blocking the door.

Elliot couldn't split his focus. The guard had a strong grip, and Elliot's only hope was to keep the gun pointed away from him. They grappled for it, but the guard wasn't giving up and Elliot couldn't get any leverage. Nabila's face appeared in his mind's eye and adrenaline surged through him. If he didn't get the gun, they were all dead, just like Nabila.

The guard pulled the gun between them and pulled the trigger. The shot went wide, but the sound reverberated through the small chamber. Elliot's ears were ringing. The guard shook his head as if his own hearing and been affected and he loosened his grip for just a second. Elliot wrenched the gun away from him. He stepped back and pointed it between the two guards.

"Stay where you are!" he shouted.

Eden turned, holding the guard's gun in her hand. She was breathing heavily and her hijab was on the floor, but she seemed to be in one piece.

"Are you okay?" The ringing had become a buzz in Elliot's ears and he was probably speaking louder than he needed to, but he wanted to make sure he could be heard.

She nodded, but motioned to Atwah with her hand. "He caught the ricochet. He's dead."

Elliot walked backward, pulling his chain with him while keeping the gun trained on the guards. Atwah had a large bloodstain on his chest that had pooled beneath him and even with ringing ears, Elliot could hear the high-pitched tone of the heart monitor that couldn't detect a heartbeat anymore. It was over.

"Let's g-get out of here." Elliot awkwardly walked toward the first guard, watching for any sudden movements, then bent and took the key ring from the man's belt. After undoing the iron chain, he rolled his ankle and took a few steps toward the door. Freedom was always a sweet feeling.

There was only one obstacle left, but before he could tell the guard to move away from the exit, a large rumble sounded overhead. The lights swung crazily, and debris began to rain down on them.

"It's caving in!" he yelled.

The guards didn't wait for any instructions. They ran into the hallway. Elliot took Eden's hand and pulled her through the doorway just as the room collapsed, the stone ceiling crashing down like an explosion as it hit the floor. Elliot tried to follow the path the guards had taken, searching his memory for all the twists and turns they'd taken through the labyrinth to get to Atwah's room. But the entire tunnel seemed to be falling down, and the hallway was quickly blocked.

Eden tugged on his hand. "This way."

She turned around and went the opposite direction. There was still rumbling overhead and adrenaline was pumping through Elliot's system so hard he could barely pull in a breath. They had to get out of there before they were buried alive. Eden ran in front of him, her long black hair streaming behind her. Elliot kept pace as they made several turns. A doctor, several nurses, and patients were running down the hallway, too, but when it forked, they chose to go down another tunnel. Eden kept going straight.

"Should we follow them?" he yelled. The other people seemed to know where they were going.

She shook her head and kept running. "Hurry!" she said over her shoulder.

The rumbling was getting louder, and the ceiling was coming down in bigger chunks. Elliot dodged a large piece, but dust rose up when it hit the floor, making him cough. Eden made one last turn around a corner and stopped. He was at her side in the next second. The tunnel was blocked.

There was no way out.

CHAPTER SIX

Eden could see a small space at the top of the stones blocking the tunnel. She tried to climb the debris to get to it, but couldn't quite make it to the top. "Give me a boost."

Elliot intertwined his fingers into a small cradle and she stepped into it, hoping her boots wouldn't hurt his hands. After getting a fingerhold on the stones, she pulled herself up and peeked out at the other side. The lights were still flickering so the generators were working at least and she could see the rest of the hallway looked fairly clear. If they could get through this barrier, they might have a chance of getting out.

"What do you see?" Elliot shifted her weight in his hands slightly, but kept her steady.

Eden bent and put her palm on his shoulder to hop down. "If we can dig through, I think we can make it out the back entrance. We've got to do it quickly, though."

Elliot looked unsure, glancing down the hall the way they'd

come. "Digging through might take some time. Should we t-try to go back out the front?"

"I think we need to get out of here as fast as we can. I'm sure the cave-in was caused by a bomb---perhaps it was dropped on us from above or maybe Amira is setting charges down here to cover her tracks. Either way, I don't think we have much time to get out alive." Eden brushed off her hands. "We just need to clear a space large enough for us to get through."

"Okay." Elliot reached up as high as he could and pushed at the barrier. "Let me see what I c-can do." He found a toehold and started up the stones as if this was a rock-climbing wall. His movements were smooth and experienced as she watched him ascend the barrier. Even in a dimly lit tunnel it was hard to miss his toned physique. His biceps strained the once-white t-shirt he was wearing and his legs were long and muscular. His body didn't seem to have an ounce of fat anywhere. He reached the top and Eden gave up trying not to stare. She watched him begin to pull down small stones and rocks with one hand. The space between the ceiling and the cave-in slowly got bigger.

"Do you need me to spell you?" Eden asked. She felt silly just watching him. There had to be something she could do.

"If I can just clear a bit more, I think you can wiggle through." His breath was coming fast. His arms had to be burning, holding his own weight and trying to move the stones.

Eden kept watch down the hall. It was eerily silent. Had everyone gotten out? Or had the last cave-in killed or trapped them? She thought of the doctor who'd been treating little Mahdi and she hoped with all of her being they'd all gotten out. *They'd been closer to the entrance so their chances were good,* she consoled herself.

Atwah's room had been near the back and Eden was grateful she'd taken the time before starting this mission to study the maze of hallways that ran through the underground hospital. Having at least two ways to exit if anything happened was always in her best interests.

After a few minutes, Elliot climbed down. He put his hands in a cradle again. "Let's get you out of here."

She rested her palms on his shoulders and looked into his eyes. Had she ever seen eyes so blue? They were the color of the sky on a beautiful summer day. "We're both getting out. Not just me."

More stones fell from the ceiling behind them and another rumble sounded overhead. A shadow of doubt crept into his gaze, but he hid it quickly and smiled. "Don't worry. I'll be right behind you."

"I'm coming back for you if you aren't."

His grip on her waist tightened. "Don't. Get yourself out no matter what happens. Don't worry about me."

Good-looking and chivalrous? It had been a long time since she'd experienced that with anyone. Or let herself even think that way about someone.

"I never leave a man behind." Her hands tightened on his shoulders, and she gave him a nod, as if that was the end of the discussion. Which it was. She took a deep breath, and he boosted her as far as he could. Eden pulled herself up the rest of the way. When she got to the top, she was surprised at how much space he'd been able to create. Pulling herself through the opening, she carefully dropped down on the other side. "Your turn," she called back.

Another explosion rippled above them and debris began

falling all around her. She dodged the bits of ceiling that were falling as rocks flew from the blockage she'd just come through and nearly knocked her down. This whole structure could go at any time.

Elliot hadn't responded and she didn't hear anything that sounded like he was starting the climb. "Elliot, is everything okay?"

There was only silence as she called his name one more time. Her stomach dropped. Had debris hit him? Was he unconscious on the other side? Anxious, she stepped forward, ready to go back, but at that moment, his face appeared at the top of the stones.

"Made it." He barely squeezed through the small space, but dropped down beside her. He was covered in dust and dirt and gingerly massaged his hand. She could see bruises on the back and his fingernails were torn. But he was with her now and she had that sense of déjà vu again, as if she'd known him before and wanted him with her.

She stared up at his face and the impulse to hug him was almost too strong to ignore. Why did she want to hug a man she'd barely met? These feelings of familiarity with him were irrational, she knew, and she didn't have time for feelings like that. She kept a tight rein on her emotions during her missions---and that's all this was. Another mission, another situation to work through. But having him beside her felt different. He had an energy around him that drew her in and made her want to get closer.

"Let's go." Tucking her thoughts away, she turned and started to walk down the hall. The emergency lights on the floor were still flickering on and off, which was a good sign.

They could help everyone trapped underground to have a chance to get out. Her gut told her they needed to hurry, though. Quickening her steps, she tried to visualize the map she'd studied before she'd come down to this godforsaken place.

Elliot was right behind her, so close she could feel his body heat. The air in the tunnel was cold, so his warmth was welcome, but it smelled faintly of smoke. Eden slowed down slightly to make sure he stayed as near as possible, resisting the urge to shiver.

"Have you been here before?" His voice echoed off the earth and stone walls. They just needed a few more minutes with no cave-ins.

"No." She stopped at a cross point that had a hallway to the right and one to the left. She took the right hallway. The exit shouldn't be that much farther now.

He looked around at the tunnel. "I'm starting to really hate enclosed spaces. I'm glad I'm not trying to figure this out alone. How do you know we're going in the right d-direction?"

He didn't seem overly anxious, and trusted her so easily. A twinge of guilt pierced her. In their business, he should know better than to trust anyone. But in this moment, she wanted to be worthy of his trust. "I always make sure I know where the emergency exits are."

"Guess I should have paid better attention." Elliot stepped over some debris on the floor and came up on her right side, his arm brushing hers. A little tingle skated down to her fingertips at his touch. Did he feel it? The current between them? She couldn't tell.

"I would think a doctor would be detail-oriented." She

glanced over at him, pressing her lips together to suppress a smile.

His eyes met hers and he raised his eyebrows. "In my defense, I was completely focused on trying not to dump my patient out of his gurney when I was brought here and we were wandering through those halls."

The corridor was just wide enough for them to walk side by side, but it was a tight fit and their shoulders and elbows touched with every step. The semi-darkness not only hid her flushed reaction to his nearness, but also provided a sense that the two of them were in a bubble that didn't include the real-world. Eden decided to embrace it for their last few moments before they made it to the exit. Why not let herself react as a woman? Just this once.

"Maneuvering a gurney? Sounds like an excuse to me," she said with a little chuckle, giving him a shoulder bump.

He stopped and touched her forearm. The warmth of his hand on her skin went right to her core, and her breath caught. She looked up at him and he leaned down until they were nearly eye-level. "Well, I did one thing right. I followed you out of that room. It helps to know the right people."

His eyes seemed to turn darker as he spoke, a blue as dark as the twilight sky. An energy she'd never felt before arced between them. What was it about this man?

"Thank you," she murmured, and immediately wished she'd said something else. What was she thanking him for? Following her?

Letting out a breath she broke their eye contact and turned, hoping he couldn't see her flush of embarrassment. The entrance appeared up ahead, and she could see David's familiar outline waiting in the shadows of the doorway. The bubble that had surrounded the two of them popped, and reality set in. It was time to get back to work.

David hurried toward them for the last few feet of the tunnel. "Are you hurt? When I heard the second and third explosions, I wasn't sure you'd make it out."

"I'm fine." She motioned toward Elliot. "We both made it out."

David didn't acknowledge Elliot and turned back toward the entrance. "We've got to go."

Eden put a bit of distance between her and Elliot, letting David be between them. The three of them exited through a small doorway. As soon as they were out of the tunnel Eden drew in a lungful of fresh evening air. The dust and grime had choked her, covering her face and clothing. She'd never forget what had happened today. Atwah. The cave-in. The closed-in feeling and the smell of burnt earth and black smoke.

David caught up to Eden and motioned down the block. "The car is over there."

Elliot started to follow them, but David turned and held up his hand. "I'm sorry, but you can't come with us. You're on your own."

Elliot stepped back, his brow furrowed. He gave her a questioning glance, but Eden wasn't sure what to say. She'd known they'd go their separate ways once they got out of the tunnels, but she didn't want to leave him, either. Whoever had dropped those bombs would want to make sure everyone in those tunnels was dead.

Elliot turned his attention back to David when she didn't

speak up. "Okay, I get it. Can you at l-least tell me exactly where I am?"

"On the outskirts of Idlib." Eden's eyes went to the sky. She could hear a helicopter and it was coming in fast. That was never good in this part of the city. "We've got to move."

They started running and found refuge in a building that was hardly more than a shell of burned-out walls and half a ceiling. All three of them watched the helicopter fly by. Eden couldn't tell which group the helicopter was from---rebels, government, ISIS, or al-Qaeda. Everyone wanted a piece of Syria right now.

"David, we can't leave him here," she whispered to her partner. "It's not safe. They'll be looking for any survivors."

"There's a situation. We can't take him with us." David touched her arm. "We've got to get back to base. We're moving out."

Elliot inched closer. "Hey, if you c-could just get me a cell phone somehow, I'll b-be out of your hair, I promise." Elliot tried to dust off his now nearly black t-shirt, but it was a lost cause. "I'm U.S. military and m-my unit is looking for me."

Eden was surprised that he'd given them that information. Was he always so trusting? She gave David a speaking glance. They were working with American partners. It wouldn't be hard to put him in touch with them.

David sighed and his shoulders slumped a little. "Fine. But he'll have to ride in the back. With a blindfold."

Eden turned back to Elliot. "I'm sure the doctor won't mind."

"As long as I know the exits f-from now on." Elliot followed them to the car and folded his long body into the small back seat. Eden slid into the passenger side while David got in the driver's seat and started the car.

"Do you have a blindfold?" Eden knew there wasn't anything in the car. It was going to be dumped when they were done with the assignment. They couldn't afford to have anything in it.

David shook his head as he looked behind them and pulled out into the road. "I guess I could rip the bottom of my shirt."

"How about I just c-close my eyes." Elliot leaned forward. "Listen, I'm not going to alert anyone to where you l-live or wherever we're going."

David pursed his lips, but didn't say anything. He was focusing on their escape, keeping to the side roads, but those were in worse condition than the main roads. Eden was bouncing in her seat so hard her teeth were rattling. With no headlights, it wasn't easy for David to see the potholes and swerve in time. It was like being tossed around at sea.

"So, are you g-guys married?" Elliot asked, shifting his weight in the back. He had to be uncomfortable in such a small car with nowhere to stretch his legs.

Eden glanced at David and chuckled. "No. We're colleagues."

"So, you're in the m-medical profession?" Elliot addressed David, who grimaced. The doctor was determined to get some information out of them. Eden had to admire the effort.

"David is more like a courier." She could hardly hold back a smile at David's grimace turning into a scowl.

"So, you deliver m-medicine? Medical care?" Elliot wasn't going to let this go.

"In a way. He delivers me to where I can best help." Eden put her hand on the dashboard, trying to hold herself steady after a particularly big bounce. The car's shocks weren't cushioning anything anymore, like they'd given up the fight as a lost cause. "He's a good helper."

"Helper? That's what you call your partner? And I have more training than you," David murmured in Hebrew. "I'm still your superior."

"Speak English," Eden admonished him softly, responding in Hebrew. "Don't make him suspicious."

Elliot sat back and folded his arms. He was quiet and Eden twisted to look at him. The little bit of moonlight coming in through the dust-covered windows illuminated his face.

"Do you want to tell me what's g-going on?" His jaw was set and the trusting look she'd seen on his face since she'd met him had disappeared. Her lungs squeezed.

"What do you mean?" Eden tried to keep her tone level. His voice had an edge to it she hadn't heard since he'd faced Amira.

"I know you're more than a n-nurse and her 'courier.'" He cleared his throat. "I may not be fluent in Hebrew, but I can understand a little. Who d-do you guys work for?" He leaned in, his shoulders barely able to fit between the front seats. "I've been in intelligence a long time. And I'd like to know who I'm dealing with. Now."

Eden glared at David. How could he have been so careless to assume an American wouldn't know Hebrew? He stared at the road, his knuckles white on the steering wheel. This was bad. Very bad.

Facing front, she closed her eyes. "I wouldn't advertise that you are U.S. military or in intelligence, Dr. Burke. I also wish you hadn't heard what you did. That changes everything. So, until we decide what's to be done with you, you'll sit back and enjoy the ride." Her voice was business-like and cold, such a contrast from their conversation in the tunnel just half an hour before. And no matter how much she wished the situation were different, they were going to have to turn him over to their commander now. He'd probably be detained.

And he wasn't going to like that.

CHAPTER SEVEN

Elliot stared at Eden's profile, her dark hair reaching below her shoulders, a frown on her lips. After that last conversation, he was seeing her in a new light, not as a capable nurse that he'd felt a connection with, but possibly as an undercover agent of some sort. Who did she work for? And where was she taking him? He rubbed the back of his neck. He'd trusted her and shouldn't have. He'd been in this business too long to give his trust so easily. But this whole mission had been a fiasco from the moment Atwah had been loaded on the plane. Being taken in by Eden was just one more disaster to add to the others. He sighed inwardly. All he needed was a phone to let Colt know where he was, and this could all be over. But with Eden's cryptic words, he probably wouldn't be getting that anytime soon.

They pulled up in front of a three-story building that looked like it had once been an apartment complex. David glanced back at him before he got out of the car and for just a moment,

Elliot thought he saw pity in his eyes. That could play to his advantage. Maybe if he felt sorry enough for him, David would just let him go.

Eden opened the back door and motioned for him to get out. "Follow me."

Her face was unemotional, her tone polite and business-like. All the warmth that had been there when she talked about her father was gone. Strangely, he missed that. He'd been enjoying being with her and that sense that he knew her somehow or had met her before had only been getting stronger. If she was in intelligence, maybe he *had* crossed paths with her at some point.

He got out and stood beside her. "Who do you work for?" he asked quietly. He needed to know. Was she with Mossad? The Syrian resistance? If he knew, he could better figure out his options. She didn't answer, so he pressed a little more. "Would your father approve of what you're doing now?"

Her features hardened at the mention of her father. "Yes, he would," she said coldly.

Turning, she started toward the building, her footsteps sure, but silent. Elliot followed and David brought up the rear. There was no electricity so the building was dark, and when they walked in the large, cavernous lobby, the shadows were longer and darker, if that was possible. Eden didn't hesitate, though, and kept walking toward a flight of stairs at the far end. Elliot briefly thought about confronting David, stealing his keys, and taking the car, but his instinct told him to see where this went. Even though he didn't know her well, his gut said Eden wasn't going to hurt him. Not to mention there really weren't many places to go as an American in Syria. He had to find a phone.

They made it to the top of the stairs and turned down a long hallway with a lot of doors. He'd thought at first it might have been an apartment building, but it could have been a hotel of some sort back in the days before the war. A few of the doors were open or hanging haphazardly from their hinges, and Elliot saw a small living area with a kitchenette to the side. Devoid of any furniture, however, the rooms just looked empty and forlorn, as if they were waiting for their old residents to return. At the end of the hall, Eden stopped in front of a door and gave a distinct knock---two taps, a pause, and three more taps. It opened and the three of them were ushered inside by a large, burly man with long sideburns and a bushy beard.

Elliot took in the room. The windows were covered with heavy canvas and temporary lights on poles were placed strategically around the room. There were two people seated at a table, tapping away at laptops. An older gentleman wearing a black suit and about the same height as David, stood near a desk on the opposite side of the room. He stared at a laptop, bending down to get closer to the screen, seemingly unaware of their presence just yet. Eden headed for him.

He turned toward her. "You've brought a guest," the man said mildly, closing the laptop as they approached. He gave Elliot a once-over.

"Couldn't be helped," Eden replied, glancing at Elliot, her face impassive. "He overheard a conversation he shouldn't have."

The older man's gaze flicked to David. "Do I want to know the specifics?"

David shifted his weight. "No, sir."

"We don't have time for this nonsense." He straightened.

"We're going to have to pass off your eavesdropper to another group. We've got business to take care of."

Whoa. Another group? Elliot stepped forward. "I just need a cell phone, sir. I can c-call my people and be out of your hair by d-daylight." He swallowed hard, wanting to control his stammer.

The man's gaze fell on him again and Elliot stared back at him. His hair was close-cropped, and his eyes were light brown and piercing. He reminded Elliot of his first commanding officer. It was like the guy could see every sin and secret you ever had. "Your people?"

"U.S. military," David supplied, an edge to his voice.

"Another complication we don't have time for." The man walked around the desk and sat down. "I need both of you here and focused. We have a job to do tonight, and we must act quickly. Take him into the other room until I can decide what to do with him." He pressed the bridge of his nose with his thumb and forefinger. "I'll need to reach out to some of my contacts."

None of this was sounding good to Elliot. "Sir, if I could just make one phone c-call, I can leave. You won't have to worry about me at all."

"Impossible." The man flicked his wrist and as soon as he did, David stepped up next to Elliot as if awaiting further command. The older man continued, "You know where we are based, you've seen our operations. We can't let you go, but you can't stay either. I need a moment to look at our options, but there are other priorities right now."

David took Elliot's arm. "Just follow orders. It's easier for everyone."

Elliot pulled away and looked at Eden. She didn't meet his gaze, but was staring at the entrance to the apartment. The guard still stood there, but nothing looked out of the ordinary. Her gaze was so intense, though, it was as if he could feel her anxiety rolling toward him.

"What is it?" he asked, furrowing his brow.

Her eyes jerked to his. "Nothing."

She was lying. Weird that he knew that. She didn't have any obvious tells like fidgeting, or looking to the right or left when she spoke. Those were all easy to spot. Eden was so good at hiding her true thoughts and emotions, yet somehow he knew she was being untruthful with him. He looked away, shaking his head slightly. His instincts had obviously gone off course where she was concerned. He'd trusted that she was who she said she was and that's what had landed him in this mess in the first place. He needed to correct his gut and whatever he thought he knew about her. Fast.

David escorted him toward a small bedroom. As he passed the two techs, he heard one tell the other how he'd missed his sister's wedding in Ofakim. Interesting. David opened the bedroom door and shoved him through before he shut it again. A cot occupied one corner with a small table, but there wasn't any other furniture. The window was covered in heavy canvas, like the ones in the living area. The apartment was a temporary base of some sort and this room was obviously a place to rest for a few hours, but nothing more. If only he knew exactly which group was using it, though he had his suspicions.

He walked the perimeter, then sat on the cot. The adrenaline was wearing off and exhaustion was starting to settle in his bones. But he couldn't rest, not yet. It was too tempting to lie down, so he stood and went to the window. Carefully drawing the canvas back, he peeked out. There were no lights from any other building, and the sky was still inky black. Looking down, he could see it was a sheer drop, so there would be no escaping through the window. Letting the canvas fall back in place, he walked to the door. Slowly pulling it open a crack, he could see Eden and David huddled with their superior. They were all staring at the laptop screen, and their expressions were drawn and serious. Whatever they were looking at wasn't good. The guard was still at the door, and the other two people hadn't moved from their places at the table. Five against one. Elliot let out a long breath. He wasn't going to escape. Not yet, anyway.

Going back to the cot, he sat down sideways on it and leaned his head against the wall. He didn't want to lie down and doze off, but sitting felt like a good compromise. Glancing around the room once more, he took stock of his situation. In the last few hours, he'd seen the most wanted terrorist in the world killed by a ricochet bullet. He'd escaped a cave-in, only to be taken prisoner again. He currently had no phone, no gun, and was waiting to be pawned off on another group. Could this get any worse?

Close on the heels of that thought he heard a high-pitched whine---a sound that had imprinted on his brain from the first time he'd heard it in Iraq. A chill went up his spine. He scrambled off the cot and ran to the door, throwing it open.

"Incoming!" he shouted, then ran toward Eden.

She met him in the middle of the room and they all ran for the doorway. Barely getting into the hall, they sprinted for the stairs when the building exploded behind them. Elliot could feel the intense heat radiating from where they'd just been. The floor rumbled beneath him. He grabbed Eden's hand and pulled her forward. They'd come this far together and he wasn't letting her go. He still had questions and he needed answers.

They rounded the corner, but before they could start down the staircase, gunfire erupted below them. Elliot immediately pulled Eden back into the hallway, but the smoke was starting to become heavy enough to clog their lungs. A fire behind them and gunmen in front.

They were trapped.

CHAPTER EIGHT

Eden was trying to take shallow breaths, sandwiched between David and Elliot, the fire behind them getting hotter and the gunmen in front of them more numerous. There wasn't much time to get out and they needed to make a move. Isaac, the head of their unit, walked calmly around them, looking like an avenging angel with his black suit and the smoke curling around his feet. He had a grenade in each hand and threw them down the stairwell.

"This way!" he shouted and seconds later the grenades exploded.

Eden clasped Elliot's hand as they both ran behind Isaac, David, the guards, and two techs bringing up the rear. Isaac's steps were sure as he led them down the hall to a fire exit. They burst through the door, inhaling large gulps of fresh air as they descended the small ladder to an alley. It wouldn't take long for the gunmen to realize where they'd gone. They needed to hurry.

"Your secondary exfil point is two blocks south and there's a car waiting. Take your new friend with you. You might need backup," Isaac said to Eden the moment he reached ground level.

"I'm her backup." David coughed as the smoke billowed into his face.

Isaac briefly turned toward David. "Your exfil point is three blocks to the north. We'll meet at the rally point in an hour." He gave instructions to the rest of the team, then he walked off at a brisk pace as everyone scattered.

"Come on," Eden told Elliot as she tugged him in the opposite direction.

Elliot was glued to her side, his eyes sweeping the area, just as Eden's were. It was a habit to take in the details of her surroundings. It looked like that was Elliot's habit as well. Not that they could see much. Darkness surrounded them. The black plumes from the building fire had obscured the moon and stars, leaving barely any light to see by. But Eden knew these streets well and had walked them in preparation for a hasty exit.

"I'd feel better if I had a gun," Elliot murmured as he shortened his stride to stay beside her.

She would prefer they both had a gun, too, but all they had right now was her handgun, which wouldn't do any good if the men with the AK-47s came out of the building and found them.

"We need to hurry," she told him, picking up speed. With the road and sidewalks so damaged in this part of town, it was dangerous to run, but she did her fastest speed walk. Elliot had no problem keeping up.

They made it to a beat-up old car and Eden climbed into the

driver's seat. Elliot got in the passenger side and kept watch as they pulled away. "Where's the rally point?" he asked, craning his neck behind him.

"On the outskirts of the city." It was their emergency backup in case they were compromised. Which, of course, they had been. How had the base been found? Had it been Atwah's people? Or another group?

The drive was silent until they were just outside Idlib. Elliot shifted in his seat and angled toward her. "I'm guessing you're Israeli intelligence."

Eden wasn't surprised he was so close to the mark. He'd gotten enough clues and he was a smart guy. She liked that about him. Her hands gripped the steering wheel tighter, but she kept her eyes on the road, hoping she hadn't given too much a reaction. "What makes you think that?"

"Just putting a few things together. Speaking Hebrew to David. You have a trace of an accent. So does Isaac. Your thoroughness with back up plans. And exits."

"Any intelligence agency would have those things," she scoffed. "That doesn't mean we're Mossad."

"But you didn't deny it." A ghost of a smile flickered over his lips.

"I didn't confirm it, either." She gave him a side-glance. "You're fishing for information."

"Maybe I want some confirmation after overhearing your techs talk about Ofakim." He was quiet for the space of a heartbeat while she processed that news. "I passed by that town once when I visited Israel."

She shook her head. Isaac would not be pleased that the guard had been so careless with information like that, but from the little she knew about Elliot, he wouldn't use what he'd heard to hurt them. "You're a well-traveled man."

He dipped his head in acknowledgment. "I imagine you are just as well-traveled."

She was, but it hadn't always been that way. "Perhaps." Had they crossed paths before? With their similar jobs, they very well could have. She was sure she would have remembered meeting someone like him, though. Why did it feel like she'd met him before?

"So was the story about your father a cover?" He shifted in his seat, peering out each window before letting his gaze rest on her again. "I understand if it was."

If only. "No, what I told you was true, actually. I haven't spoken of my family in a very long time." She could hear surprise in her voice. In her line of work, it would be dangerous to share personal details like that. But something about Elliot drew her to him, made her less cautious. That was dangerous and she knew it. Her training told her to stay away from him, but like a bee to nectar, she couldn't resist being near him for as long as possible.

"I'm sorry about your dad," Elliot said softly.

Eden nodded. What could she say? She pulled the car into a stall inside a small parking complex that was mostly still standing. This part of town had obviously been bombed at one point with all the damage around them. Hopefully the building wouldn't collapse with their car inside it. She put her fingers on the door handle. "Stay close."

"I plan to." His voice was like velvet, with that little half-smile on his lips as he looked at her. For a split second, she wanted to stay in the car with him. To talk. To learn more about each other. But she was there to do a job, and in reality, he wasn't part of it, even though he was currently tagging along. She had to keep her head in the game.

They exited the car and moved down the parking complex stairs, keeping close to the side of the building. This was more of an industrial area, with a large warehouse up ahead. Eden walked quickly to the warehouse side door, with Elliot on her right. She could feel his constant visual sweeps as he looked for danger, and it was comforting to know she had someone there to watch her back. She slipped inside and stood for a moment while her eyes adjusted to the dark. A small light switched on in the middle of the building and flickered twice. That was their signal that it was safe. Eden moved toward where the light had come from.

A group of offices were on the far wall, and as Eden's eyes adjusted to the small bit of light, she could see the shadows more clearly. Isaac was here. So was David. And another man was with them. What had happened to the rest of their team? Isaac probably sent them to another location. She didn't want to think of the alternative. It was better to believe they had all made it out safely. Taking a breath, she walked to the door and opened it, holding it for Elliot. He kept close to her side as she made her way into the room and then he went to the nearest corner where he could observe.

Isaac was busy at a small office table, pouring some coffee from a thermos into cups. He turned to hand her one, lifting his chin as they entered. "Good to see you both made it. We've got a lot to do."

Eden nodded, but part of her was confused. Was he including Elliot in the mission then?

Isaac's eyes flickered to Elliot's and he offered him a cup of coffee as well before he spoke.

"The rest of the team is setting up a base ops at our secondary location. We won't be without tech or satellite imagery for long." It was as if Isaac could read her thoughts and knew she'd worried about them. Eden was glad they were all safe.

Isaac gestured to the man on the other side of him. "And now for the reason we are all here. Luke has some new information about Amira that we need to act on immediately."

The other man was dressed in nearly the same clothes as Eden---a black t-shirt, black pants, and black boots---only his looked a lot cleaner than hers did. She'd done her best to get the grime and dust off, but it was pretty much a lost cause.

Luke stepped forward. His clothes were clean, but he was looking a little more scruffy than when she'd seen him last, his dark hair long enough to curl around his collar and his jaw sporting a few days' worth of beard growth. He would be able to blend into the background in almost any situation, though, which was probably what he wanted. Eden respected Luke, and so far the intel he'd provided them had been solid. He met her eyes, his expression serious. Whatever he was about to say wouldn't be good news.

"When we received the intel from Eden that Amira had taken Atwah's fingerprints before he was killed, we started looking into what she would need his fingerprints for and came up with one thing. She wants entrance into the Council of Seven."

There was dead silence in the room as they all digested the news. Eden's eyes snapped to Isaac's. Had he known? They'd long suspected the Council of Seven was real, a consolidation of power that included seven of the terrorist groups in the region, but they could never get any proof. "How do you know that? Most people think the Council of Seven is a myth." She folded her arms and waited for Luke's answer.

He smiled slightly. "We have a highly placed source that has personally witnessed the heads of seven terrorist organizations secretly form this council. They consult regularly and we were informed that they've now made the Council of Seven their central command. As you can imagine, having that kind of organization makes them more powerful and their threat to the free world more real."

More real and more dangerous. So many thoughts raced through Eden's mind. "How long have you known about it? And what's been done to stop them?" Were the Americans sitting on this information?

"We got confirmation of their new central command and then our source reported the Council of Seven called a meeting six days from now. They'll be replacing Atwah on their council. The meeting is sort of like a job interview, if you will, and Amira is their top candidate. She's anxious to be seen as a viable leader and she is mounting an attack as we speak on the al-Sina'a prison. There are hundreds of ISIS and al-Qaeda fighters there. She wants to break them out to form her own army."

Elliot took a step forward. "We can't let that happen. Are there p-plans in place to counter her attack?"

Luke turned his head to look at him and then nodded in acknowledgment. "We've been working on a plan and have called in some of our best assets." He looked around the room at each of them. "The plan includes all of you here of course."

"If you've c-called in the best, that means Griffin Force is on its way." Elliot moved a bit closer to Luke. "Because if I'm not m-mistaken, you're CIA, and if the CIA is partnering with Mossad, you've probably looped in MI6, as well. They all have assets here, but no one has more of a n-network in Syria than Griffin Force." He met Luke's gaze head-on.

Luke raised his eyebrows. "Well, you got most of it right. We have partnered with Mossad in the past, but you have the pleasure of being in the company of the Chol group tonight---former Mossad officers who've done a lot of good in the world."

Elliot was with Griffin Force? That explained a lot. They were the elite when it came to tracking down terrorists. But Eden was surprised Luke had given information out about Chol. Isaac hadn't stopped him, though, so Elliot must have been vetted and approved somehow. She watched Elliot closely for any reaction, but he hadn't given a visible one. He was probably just happy he'd be reunited with Griffin Force soon.

"I've heard of Chol," Elliot said. "The reports have been pretty impressive." He lifted his eyes to meet Eden's and his lips turned up at the corners. "Their operatives are trained well."

Eden gave him a small smile in return, then sipped her coffee. Everything seemed a little brighter in her world now that he knew who they were and was apparently an accepted part of the team.

Luke looked between Eden and Elliot, his eyebrows raised. "Yeah, Chol is impressive, Griffin Force is great, but this old CIA guy has a pretty good network in Syria, too, just so you know. That's how we're doing all this intelligence gathering."

"I mean I didn't want to call you old, but since you're aware . . ." Elliot lifted a shoulder in a half-shrug as his voice trailed off.

Luke laughed outright. "I'm sure Griffin Force will be happy to see you, Dr. Burke. They've used every contact they had to get information on your whereabouts."

Elliot let out an audible sigh. "And I'll be glad to see them." He finished off his coffee and put his cup down on the table near the thermos.

Luke turned back to include Isaac and David. "We're meeting Griffin Force and a few other friends near the prison. It's pretty much all hands-on deck for this mission. If Amira breaks any of those prisoners out, she'll have the power and influence to take over for her father. And no one wants that to happen. Amira is just as callous as Atwah---if not more so."

"Any questions?" Isaac asked.

Eden didn't have any questions so she finished her coffee and set her cup next to Elliot's.

Elliot cleared his throat. "While we were in the tunnels, I overheard Amira talking about meeting with an arms dealer. He wants his money ASAP and from what I could tell, whatever weapon he's selling is expensive." Elliot shook his head. "If she has weapons *and* an army, we're going to have our hands f-full."

Luke let out a breath. "I've heard a bit of chatter, but nothing concrete. How sure are you?"

"I was standing five feet away when she was talking to her second-in-command about it. I'm sure."

"Okay, we'll make sure that's passed along." Luke nodded to him as he turned to leave. "Thanks."

Elliot was about to follow him, but Eden put out her hand. "Are you sure you're up for this? You've been through a tunnel collapse and a bombing already today. No one would blame you if you needed to stay back and wait to rejoin your team."

Elliot grinned so wide, a little dimple appeared in his cheek. "I wouldn't miss this for anything in the world. I've been chasing Atwah for more than a year, and now that he's dead, we have a chance to stop Amira and cut off the head of the snake. I'm going to be right there when it happens."

"We both will." Eden tilted her head. He impressed her. The way he handled himself. His can-do attitude. She felt the same way about being there when Amira was captured. There was no way she'd want to be sidelined for this op no matter what she'd been through. They walked through the door and into the warehouse. It felt good to be sharing this mission with him. Right, somehow. She couldn't explain it.

Isaac cleared away the thermos and cups, putting them into a duffel bag. He moved to a large metal locker and unlocked it, handing out the weapons and tactical gear stashed inside. Eden watched Elliot check his and familiarize himself with the grip of the gun. He was focused and intense as he readied to do battle. Eden could hardly take her eyes off him, her middle doing a little flip. She'd never found anyone she connected with more and if they lived through this, she wanted a chance to explore that feeling. She tore her gaze away from Elliot and took the gun Isaac handed her. They walked toward the exit as a group, primed for what was ahead.

It was going to be a long night.

CHAPTER NINE

Elliot sat in the backseat of the van with Eden, playing with the earpiece in his hand. He hadn't inserted it yet, as if putting it off would somehow delay the fight in front of them, but there was no stopping what was coming. They had a chance to end a new generation of terrorism, but there were a lot of variables they couldn't predict. With a sigh, he finally just put it in his ear. Folding his arms, he had to work to keep his foot from bouncing. Whenever he went into battle, he always had an excess of nervous energy. This time was no different.

"Anxious to see your team?" Eden shifted toward him. The interior of the van was dark, but the farther they traveled, the brighter the moon was, making her eyes seem luminous. She'd hastily put her hair into a bun back at the warehouse. He could still see traces of yellowish dust streaking through it from the stones of the tunnel cave-in. One piece of hair had already fallen forward, though, skimming her cheek. Elliot was tempted to reach out and tuck it behind her ear, but he resisted the urge.

Pulling his thoughts back to the present, he remembered she'd asked him a question. "Yeah, I'm sure they've b-been worried about me." He leaned in closer and got a whiff of cinnamon. Was she wearing some sort of perfume? Or had she eaten something with cinnamon earlier? He inhaled one more time. "Sounds like you'll be working with me for a while longer, though."

Eden gave him a half-smile as she put in her earpiece. "'Working together' might be a bit of a stretch. You've mostly been tagging along."

Elliot chuckled softly, appreciating her directness. Now that it had been revealed who everyone worked for, he was on more solid footing with her, and deep down he was glad. He couldn't remember the last time he'd found so much enjoyment just talking to a woman. "That's one way to put it."

The darkness outside the van was suddenly lit up like a nuclear sunrise when a huge ball of fire erupted about a mile in front of them.

Luke's voice shouted into their earpiece, "Hurry! Truck bomb on the prison north wall. Blew a hole big enough for a platoon to escape from."

David sped up the van and within seconds they were about a mile from the prison. "Be careful," he said to the group as he got out and shut the door.

Jogging toward the fire, their team took up defensive positions a half mile from the prison entrance. Bursts of gunfire were starting to echo all around them. Elliot gripped his gun and glanced over at Eden. She was standing nearly the same way he was, ready for anything with her tac vest on and a gun in her hand. For just a second, he had déjà vu, as if he'd seen her like this before.

Another explosion sounded behind them, strong enough to rock the ground beneath their feet, immediately pulling his complete attention to the mission at hand. "What are they blowing up?" Elliot said out loud. Heavy smoke started to drift toward their position.

"Two oil tankers are on fire." Luke's voice over the earpiece was eerily calm, as if he were merely passing along last night's sports score. "Delta group, we're heading to you now. Hold your positions."

Elliot visually swept the area while they waited for Luke's group to join them, his eyes coming back to rest on Eden. She was still in a ready position. It hardly seemed possible that he'd known her less than forty-eight hours. They'd saved a terrorist's life under duress, survived a near cave-in, a bombing, and now they were about to confront ISIS fighters. And in all of those situations, she'd been unruffled and focused. She was obviously good at her job. But she'd given him a glimpse of who she was when she wasn't working, and he couldn't stop going back to those little impressions. Her soft smile when she talked about her dad. Her dry humor. There was something about her that intrigued him. And he still had that feeling of familiarity whenever he was near her. He had to have met her before, that was the only explanation. Once this was all over, he hoped they'd have a bit of time to explore all of that before another mission came up.

The gunfire around the prison was intensifying, and their window to do anything about it was quickly closing. Elliot wanted to ask where Luke was, but then he appeared in the darkness, walking with Colt. Nate, Brenna, Abby, and Jake brought up the rear.

Gratitude and relief filled him. Elliot lowered his weapon and hugged Colt, then Brenna, Abby, Nate, and Jake. "I can't even tell you how glad I am to see you guys. Took you long enough to g-get here."

"Next time let me know before you take time off to tour Syria." Colt grinned, but his eyes were giving Elliot a once-over, as if to check for obvious injury.

"Copy that." Elliot chuckled and pulled away, glad to be back with his team---his family. There'd been a few instances over the last two days where he really thought that this could be it and he'd never see them again. He was glad he'd been wrong. He was stronger with his team at his back and reuniting with them boosted the chances for mission success, not to mention Elliot's personal peace of mind. He turned to Nate. "I'm just going to say that with your c-concussion, you definitely shouldn't be in the field."

"Couldn't let you guys have all the fun. I feel fine." Nate lifted his chin toward the prison. "We need to shut this all down while we can."

Abby shook her head. "We all told him the same thing, El. He's stubborn."

That earned a laugh from all of them. Luke stepped forward, breaking up their little reunion. "The Syrian Defense Forces are taking heavy fire from the outside, and a prison riot is creating chaos inside. We can't get any air support because of the smoke from the tankers. Our three teams will join the SDF and make sure no high-level terrorist leaders escape."

"Outnumbered and no air support? That's an easy d-day for Griffin Force," Elliot said with a grin for his team leader.

"Oh, yeah." Colt put his hands on his hips and nodded in agreement. "We got this."

Luke spoke into his throat mic. "We're making a perimeter around the prison. Delta group to the east, Echo to the north, and Alpha to the west. SDF teams are on point."

They moved out and Eden kept pace running alongside him. They were all front-focused as they approached the prison. A pickup truck burned next to a large gaping hole in the concrete wall, and Elliot caught a glimpse of men kneeling in the yard. Maybe the SDF had a handle on things already. Luke headed through a wire fence, and Delta team followed.

Men were in groups throughout the yard, some in hand-to-hand combat with prison guards and others running away. "Form a perimeter around the wall," Luke ordered.

Elliot went to his left and saw a man heading for the hole in the wall the truck bomb had created. Running after him, Elliot yelled, "Stop!"

The man looked back at him. Small eyes and a pointy chin that boasted a long, scraggly beard. A mouth that had a gold front tooth gleaming in the light from the fires. Elliot recognized that face. It was Abu Hamza al-Hashimi, a top tier, ISIS leader. Elliot raised his gun. "Stop, or I'll shoot!" He squeezed the trigger, but aimed for the ground at al-Hashimi's feet. The bullet pinged mere inches from his heels. He stopped and faced Elliot, a toothy smile on his face.

Elliot approached the man carefully, but didn't see any other weapons on him. He kept his gun trained on al-Hashimi until he'd patted him down. Forcing him to kneel, Elliot zip-tied al-Hashimi's hands. "Stay put."

Elliott stayed close, but scanned the prison yard. He finally found her. Eden was about fifty feet away, grappling with a man at least a head taller than her. Elliot started over in case she needed help, but in a split-second Eden flipped the guy on his back and had her gun pointed at his chest. A flare of pride went through him. She could hold her own.

Wiping the sweat from his face, he looked around and saw the majority of prisoners raising their hands in surrender. SDF had clearly gained the upper hand. But something wasn't sitting well with Elliot. They'd all given up too easily for men who had a good chance of escape, especially with help from the outside. He stalked back to al-Hashimi who was still kneeling on the ground where Elliot had left him.

"This is a pretty pathetic prison break," Elliot said as he approached. "You d-didn't even make it past the outer wall."

Al-Hashimi lifted his head, that annoying smile still on his face, but he said nothing.

Elliot stood over him, watching for any reactions that could give him a clue as to what buttons to push to get him to talk. "I know you speak English. I was there when you were captured in Raqqa. You made a pathetic attempt to escape there, too." Elliot crouched down and looked into al-Hashimi's eyes. "We had you t-trapped like a rat in those underground tunnels."

"T-t-t-trapped? Having a hard time getting your lies out?" Al-Hashimi mocked Elliot's stutter, then spit in his face. "We will have revenge for everything you have taken from us. And then we will see who is trapped like a rat."

His little dig didn't bother Elliot. He wiped the spit from his cheek and chuckled a bit. "Oh yeah? How's the revenge game going? Looks to me l-like you've lost again."

That calculating smile appeared on his face again. "I think not."

Those words sent chills up Elliot's spine. Was this a trap? Elliot straightened as Colt and Luke joined him. "You remember Abu Hamza al-Hashimi?" Elliot motioned to the man kneeling in front of them. "He seems to think they're w-winning here."

Cursing softly, Luke stared down at the prisoner. He turned and spoke quietly into his SAT phone. Elliot couldn't quite hear what he was saying, but from the look on his face, he'd figured something out. And it was bad.

Colt met his eyes and shrugged. They both turned to look at the yard. Even through the smoke, they could see that the prison break had been suppressed. Guards stood over the prisoners and the yelling and gunfire had stopped. That should be a good thing, but Elliot had a sinking feeling in his gut.

Eden joined them, wiping the blood from a small cut on her cheek. Elliot leaned in to get a look at the wound, but she waved him away. "I'm fine," she told him. "What's going on?"

With one last look at al-Hashimi to make sure he was secure, Elliot moved closer to Luke. Colt and Eden followed. Luke had a death-grip on the SAT phone, as if he was trying to stop himself from throwing it. His lips were pursed tight, barely more than a line slashing across his face as he listened. David, Nate, Brenna, Abby, and Jake joined them, and they all formed a circle around Luke as he disconnected the call.

"This was too easy." Colt blew out a breath. "The prison break was the distraction, wasn't it?"

Luke clenched his jaw as if he didn't want to give the answer. He glanced around the group. "They kept us busy here, while the real prison break was at al-Shaddadi." He ran a hand over his face. "About 100 ISIS fighters escaped. Looks like they headed out on side roads between al-Shaddadi and al-Hol and are likely going toward the Tuwaiman desert. We're going to try to head them off."

"Any s-sign of Amira?" Elliot asked, dread pooling in his gut. This was bad. Very bad.

"She was in the lead car." Luke's tone was grim. "This was well-planned and well-executed. She broke out two ISIS generals and their finance chief, as well as Atwah's uncle. That's going to look great on her resume when she meets with the Council of Seven."

Eden stepped forward, her chin thrust out. "Not if we recapture them before they disappear." She held Luke's gaze. "We can do this, but we've got to move now."

Elliot looked at the determination on her face. She wasn't going to sit around and bemoan what had happened. She was ready to go and he was, too. "You heard the lady."

"Okay, then." Luke nodded. He reached for the SAT phone again, but Abby reached out and held his forearm.

"I'm not sure if you remember meeting me years ago," she said to Luke. "But I've got a few contacts in Syria that might be able to help."

"I rarely forget a face and you're pretty much a legend," he told her with a polite smile. "But I have some transportation on standby. We can be there before sunup and start scouring every inch of that desert." Abby nodded and started to move back.

"You know, we had the same handler at the CIA once. I'd like to compare notes sometime."

"I'd like that." Abby gave him a short nod in agreement.

The group huddled closer for a second, as if they were a sports team ready to storm the field. Elliot had always had that sense of camaraderie with Griffin Force, but adding Eden and Luke, even David, being there felt right. He grinned as he looked at the faces in the circle. "Go, team!"

They all smiled as they turned to head for the exit point. Eden fell into step beside him.

"How's the cheek?" he asked her.

"Just a scratch."

"Let's keep an eye on it. We don't w-want any infections." Elliot went through the wire gate first, then turned to wait for her.

"Are you always this much of a worrywart?" She holstered her gun as she walked, as if it was the most natural thing in the world to her. Which it probably was in her line of work.

"Yes, I'm definitely a worrywart." He glanced over at her. "But my p-patients tell me it's part of my bedside charm."

She laughed. "Well, I agree with them."

Eden gave him a wide smile and held his gaze for a long moment. Elliot's pulse began to pound, and it definitely wasn't from adrenaline. Luke's voice cut through the unspoken conversation between them, calling for her. She broke eye contact with a tilt of her head and jogged forward. Elliot watched her go.

She was a warrior who'd been bloodied, but she was all in to finish the fight. He liked the idea of working together to bring down Amira. Even though they barely knew each other, his mind raced toward possibilities. She could be a true partner on and off the battlefield and that was something he'd never thought he'd have.

But having something meant you could lose it, and in a war, that was almost inevitable. Risking his heart right now would be foolish, but watching her talk with Luke, he really wanted to---and knew he couldn't.

CHAPTER TEN

Eden leaned her head against the van window and closed her eyes for a moment. The drive to the Tuwaiman desert had been a silent one, each member of the team lost in their thoughts or taking a power nap. That was one of the things she'd learned first in the field---sleep when you can. But today her thoughts wouldn't let her relax enough to sleep. How had Amira pulled off breaking out such high-level prisoners? Why had their intel not picked up even a whisper of what was really happening?

They'd go over all of that in debrief. Right now they needed to focus on how to stop Amira and the men she'd broken out before they made it to the desert. Once they got there, tracking them would be nearly impossible. All of the escaped prisoners knew the area well and had disappeared there many times. Their uncanny ability to vanish was one of the reasons it had been so difficult to capture them in the first place.

Eden lifted up a hand and put her fingers to the wound on

her cheek. Now that the adrenaline was wearing off, her face was starting to throb where she'd been struck. She wished she had an ice pack or something. Her cheek felt like it was on fire.

Elliot reached into his medical bag and took out a small square. He twisted it and handed it to her. "You're g-going to have a nice bruise. I bet an ice pack would help."

Her fingers brushed his as she took it from him and a tingle of warmth went through her. Was he always so attuned to the people around him? That was probably what made him a good doctor. She hoped he didn't have any mind-reading abilities, considering how many thoughts she'd had of him. "Thanks."

The SAT phone next to her buzzed, and she picked it up. "Hello."

Luke's voice sounded in her ear. "One of the generals has been spotted in al-Shaddadi. We're setting up a perimeter. Head to these coordinates." He rattled off some numbers. "Stay alert. We don't want him slipping past us."

Eden passed along the coordinates to David, and he pressed on the accelerator. They had a lead. If they could recapture one of the generals, maybe they could get him to talk and give some information that could lead to Amira. Realistically, that probably wouldn't happen, but they could get lucky this time. Maybe the general was tired of prison, and they could cut him a deal.

They arrived at al-Shaddadi in record time. The sun was barely above the horizon and the streets were quiet, but there was an air of anxiousness in the city, as if the people knew something was coming and they wanted to stay inside to avoid it. When they were close to the coordinates Luke had given them, they got out of the car and went the last little bit on foot.

Colt met up with them near the perimeter line around the target building.

"Glad you all made it." He wiped a bit of sweat from his brow. Even though the mornings were cooler, it was still warm, especially with all of their equipment on.

"Any sign of the general?" Eden asked, adjusting her tactical vest.

"Not yet. We think he's holed up over there." Colt pointed to a small house down the street. The windows were all closed, the shutters drawn over them.

"Anyone else home?" Elliot asked, rubbing a hand over the scruff on his jaw. Even though he'd been awake for nearly forty-eight hours, he still looked fairly presentable and ready to go. Eden glanced away. She could only imagine what she looked like right now. She'd never really cared about her appearance in the field before, but today she wished she could at least wash her face and get some of the grime off.

"There are two heat signatures in the house. We're gathering intel on the homeowner." Colt's brow furrowed as he stared down the street. "This feels like a stall tactic to keep us standing around. The longer we wait, the more time Amira and the rest of the prisoners have to escape to where we'll never find them."

David shook his head as soon as Colt mentioned Amira's name. "I'm sure our combined teams are all keeping an eye out for Amira and the rest of the escapees. There's no way anyone is letting them go so easily." His tone was curt and defensive.

Colt put up a hand at David's outburst. "Hey, I know we're all doing our best here. We all want the same thing. Something just feels off."

Eden walked to David's side and closed her fingers around

his arm. His bicep tensed under her touch. He stared intently at the house, barely acknowledging her presence.

"Why would the general pick that house?" he said softly, as if musing to himself.

Eden's gaze followed his. "It was convenient? He knew the homeowner was a sympathizer?"

"General Rakawi is a brilliant strategist. He wouldn't let himself be cornered like this." David tilted his head. "There has to be another reason." His eyes skittered over to Luke. "Maybe we got bad intel and he's not even there."

Eden pressed her lips together and stared at the house, her mind mulling over David's words. She thought Luke's intel was probably good, but David had a point. Why this house? She started walking down the street toward it. "We need to see inside that house."

"Hey," Luke called out to her.

Eden shook her head. "Don't worry. I can do this," she said over her shoulder.

When she got closer, she could hear the murmur of voices coming from the security perimeter, but Luke or Colt must have said something. Everything got quiet. Her entire focus was on the house in front of her. She was beginning to doubt the general was there. Amira had played them before. With the extensiveness of the distraction tactic that had taken them to the wrong prison, it was reasonable to think Amira had planned the real prison break down to the last detail. The general wouldn't be so stupid as to hole up in a little house near the center of town.

The back of the house boasted a small courtyard, and she easily vaulted over the low concrete wall. Keeping her gun at the ready, she crept closer to the window near the back door. She peeked over the edge and saw a child standing next to a woman who was sitting at a table, her back to Eden. There was no one else present that she could see. A crunch of gravel sounded behind her and she raised her gun. Elliot held up his hands, quietly joining her.

He took up position behind her. His presence was reassuring as they moved nearly as one toward the back door. If the general wasn't in the kitchen near the woman and her child, perhaps they could breach and give her a way out, then go in and get the general. If he really was inside. The closer she got, the more she thought Colt was right. Something felt off.

They made it to the back door and Eden wasn't surprised to see it was booby-trapped. Colored wires ran all the way around it and were connected to a brick of C4. If they opened it, the explosion would kill them, the woman, and her child. Eden sucked in a breath. Defusing bombs wasn't one of her skills.

Elliot moved around her, his eyes focused on the wires. He took a pair of pliers from his tac vest and began a closer look at the explosive device.

"Do you have experience disarming bombs?" she whispered, watching his fingers move over the wires as he assessed how the bomb was put together.

"Don't worry. I've got steady hands." He glanced at her, a flash of humor in his eyes.

She couldn't help the corners of her mouth ticking up into a smile. "Steady hands won't matter if you clip the wrong wire," she told him with a quirk of her eyebrow.

"Trust me."

She did trust him, which surprised her a little, considering they barely knew each other. But she innately knew he would never deliberately hurt her. And they needed to get in that house. If the general was in there, this was their chance to grab him. If he wasn't, they needed to come up with an alternate plan to recapture him.

Eden hardly dared to breathe as she watched his hands pass over each wire. Finally, he chose one and pulled it away from the rest.

"Here we go," he whispered as he clipped the wire.

Eden waited another three heartbeats. No explosions. They were still here. He'd chosen the right one.

Carefully opening the door, she slowly went to the woman's side, her senses on alert.

"Be very quiet," Eden said in Arabic. The woman pulled her child to her, pressing his head to her chest, but she stayed silent. "Is there a man here?"

The woman shook her head. Her eyes lowered to the rug near the fireplace. Elliot kicked the rug to the side. A trap door.

"Tunnels," he groaned. "We should have known." He turned on his comms. "Delta Leader, the target has escaped into a t-tunnel. We're going to see where it leads. We'll probably lose c-communication while we're underground."

"Copy that," Luke replied. "Be careful."

Elliot checked for any more boobytraps, then pulled on the ring attached to the top of the wooden door. It creaked open, revealing a dark hole cut into the earth. He grimaced and took out his small flashlight to check the space he could see. Eden looked over his shoulder. No one appeared to be anywhere near the entrance. Elliot bent and gripped the edge before lowering himself down. Eden waited a few moments, then dropped down beside him. The flashlight curbed the darkness for a few feet in front of them. He clicked it off.

"What are you doing?" she whispered, but even that bit of sound carried in the silence.

"Letting my sense of hearing t-tell me if anyone is close."

Eden stood at his side and listened as well. Nothing moved. Elliot turned the light back on. She nodded and they started forward.

The tunnel was dirt and stone, likely hand-carved, considering the tool marks and piles of dirt on the ground every few feet. Whoever had built it had lost motivation halfway through since it had started wide and well-made, but then narrowed so much it was difficult for even one person to walk in without hunching over. From the broken cobwebs on the ceiling and walls, however, it was easy to see someone had recently come through here.

The only sound was their puffs of breath as they made their way to the end, where another trap door waited in the ceiling. Elliot cautiously climbed the small wooden ladder to open it, his gun at the ready. Eden moved to the other side to back him up. Elliot slowly opened the door and scrambled through it as quickly as possible. Eden followed. It was a storage room filled with crates---and the general wasn't anywhere to be seen. Eden moved to the doorway and moved aside the curtain covering it.

"Where are we?" he asked her, keeping his voice low.

"From the looks of it, we're in the back of a clothing shop." Brightly colored handmade shirts were displayed on several different sizes of wooden shelves. She let the curtain drop. "The front faces the *souk* and I don't see anyone else nearby. Coming through here is a convenient way to get lost in the crowds at the market." She walked forward and inspected some of the crates. "And a great place for the general to change out of his prison jumpsuit." She held up the blue uniform for prisoners. "At least we can confirm he was here."

"Yeah, but where is h-he now? That's the question of the day." Elliot went to the back exit and looked out into the alley.

Their comms crackled to life. "Any sign of the target?" Luke asked.

"No, but we're in pursuit." Elliot put his hand to his ear. "Can you track us on satellite?"

"Affirmative. Back up is on its way."

Elliot held out his hand to Eden. "Let's see if we can figure out which way he went."

She didn't hesitate and took his hand as they moved into the alley, enjoying the contact for a moment before squeezing his fingers and letting go to pull out her gun. His touch grounded her somehow, calmed her for the fight to come.

The sound of motorbikes and people talking together got louder the more they walked. Eden turned the corners toward the *souk* carefully, knowing instinctively that was the direction the general would go. The heart of the market was close, the noise of those who came to barter and sell making it hard to hold a conversation. She craned her neck over the crowd of people in front of her. Slowly scanning for anyone that was wearing a shirt like those she'd seen in the clothing shop, she quickly found a man wearing one of the colorful garments. From his height and bearing, it had to be the general. He was making his way to the street, looking over his shoulder as he went.

"There he is." Hoping Elliot could hear her over the crowd,

she motioned with her arm and started forward. Elliot was right behind her.

The crowd seemed to close in around them. Eden holstered her gun and pushed through as forcefully as she could, saying 'excuse me' in Arabic. Elliot was doing the same. She didn't want to lose the general and each precious second counted. Just as they reached the corner where they'd seen him last, a motorcycle revved loudly and barreled toward them. Elliot pulled Eden to him, shielding her body with his own, as he jumped out of the way and the motorcycle shot past, barely missing them. They fell to the ground, hard, just as an explosion sounded behind them. Black smoke and high-pitched screaming filled the air.

Eden lay motionless underneath him, her eyes closed. Her head hurt, and unconsciousness swirled close, waiting to pull her under.

"Hey, are you okay?" Elliot asked, his voice sounding very far away.

She wanted to answer him, but the darkness pulled too hard. "I'm sorry," she wanted to say. But no words came.

CHAPTER ELEVEN

Eden wanted to keep her eyes closed. Her head ached and she was so tired. But when the smell of smoke finally registered, she remembered the general getting away on a motorcycle and tossing a grenade as he blew past them. Once her brain reminded her of that, the sounds all around her also appeared, the screaming and groaning. And then there was Elliot.

His voice was soft, but urgent. "Eden."

She opened her eyes to see him peering down into her face. His forehead was creased with worry and she wanted to reach up and touch his cheek, to reassure him that she was okay, but any type of movement seemed like a monumental task.

"Still here," she said, her voice little more than a croak.

"Thank heavens for that." His hands cupped the back of her head and slowly moved forward. "You've got a bit of a g-goose egg on the side of your head. I can't see any other wounds, though. Does it hurt anywhere else?"

Eden took stock of her aches and pains. "Just bruises, I think. Nothing is horribly painful except my head."

Elliot let out a little breath as if he'd been holding it, waiting for her answer. "Good." He straightened just in time to see Colt running toward them.

"You okay?" he asked when he neared.

"Yeah, we're okay. The general had a m-motorcycle hidden around that corner. Threw a grenade on his way by." Elliot wiped his brow, assessing the wounded around him. "We're going to need some emergency services right away for the injured."

"Already taken care of." Luke appeared next to Colt. "We've got a bead on the general. He's not getting away that easily."

Eden sat up very slowly, trying to clear her head. She looked around at the alley, a hole in the back of the building next to them from the grenade blast, and some bystanders still on the ground with various wounds. She took in some deep breaths to give herself a moment to get her bearings. That helped a little. Elliot stayed close, watching her with a concerned look in his eyes. She put her hand on what was left of the wall of the building next to her and got to her feet, but her legs felt a little wobbly. Elliot took her elbow, and though she didn't want to show him any weakness, she was grateful for the support.

"Can we intercept him?" She wouldn't mind getting in the interrogation room with the general. There were a few things she'd like to say to his face about how cowardly he'd been since his prison escape. Hiding behind an innocent woman and her child. Detonating an explosive in a market with innocent civilians. He wouldn't care what she thought of his actions, but it would make her feel better to say it.

"Our satellite picked him up and we're tracking him. We've got a perimeter set up around the city, so it's just a matter of time. Then we'll take him to the safehouse." Luke looked at his phone, his brows knitting together as he stared at his screen.

"It won't be as easy as it sounds," Elliot said, his mouth pulling down into a frown. "He's a seasoned soldier. And he knows how to disappear."

"Not this time. As soon as we had his location, we knew he'd try to flee the city. We've been waiting for him." Luke took another glance at his phone and smiled. "We had spike strips ready on the road and the general went down like a brick. They're loading him into the truck now."

That was music to Eden's ears, but those same ears were still ringing a bit. She leaned a little harder on Elliot's arm, a wave of dizziness overtaking her. The action was enough for his attention to snap back to her.

"You okay?" he said, his voice low.

"Fine," she whispered back. They both knew it was a lie, but she couldn't exactly say otherwise when they were in the field.

"We'll rally at the safehouse," Luke told them. He put his SAT phone to his ear and took a few steps away. Colt followed but turned to wait for Elliot and Eden.

"A bit of a close call there," Colt said as they slowly made their way back to the car. Eden tried to walk at a normal pace, but the dizziness slowed her down. She leaned on Elliot's arm more than she wanted to, but there was no helping it. If she didn't, she might fall over. The men didn't say anything, but she could feel their eyes on her.

"We've had a few close c-calls in the last forty-eight hours,"

Elliot said. "I'm starting to forget what it's like to not be running for my life five times a day."

Eden let out a huff of laughter.

"Hopefully we're turning a corner with that," Colt said as they met up with Jake and the others. "Augie is here now, too, and he'll hopefully be able to help us get eyes on Amira."

"If anyone can do it, Augie can." Elliot helped Eden into the waiting car, and then climbed in after her. She leaned her head back against the seat while Elliot filled the others in on what had happened. Eden listened, very aware that she was pressed close to his side from shoulder to hip. It was tempting to just lay her head on his shoulder and close her eyes, but that wouldn't be appropriate while on a mission. She couldn't remember the last time she'd slept or eaten, and her body was letting her know she had to take care of those things. Soon, if not immediately.

Elliot continued with his report, his stammer hardly noticeable. He controlled it well. The tone of his voice soothed her, so while she couldn't lay her head on him, she closed her eyes and let his words rumble through her. What was it about this man that was so comforting?

They arrived at the safehouse. Elliot kept close to her side. Once they'd gone through the back door, he asked Luke for a room so he could examine her. "She was injured in the market, and I just want to make sure she's really okay."

Luke peered into her face, and she must have looked pale or something because he nodded right away. "Third door on the right."

Part of Eden wanted to protest, tell them she was fine, but she didn't. Maybe having Elliot give her a clean bill of health was the best way to convince them she didn't need to be taken out of the field.

She allowed Elliot to lead her to the room and she sat on the bed. Elliot pulled a chair up next to her. "Tell me exactly where your injuries are, and don't downplay anything. I want to hear about every bruise, no matter how small."

She gave him a half-smile. "A little bossy, no?"

"This is my firm voice for stubborn patients," he said as he lifted her wrist to take her pulse.

His fingers were warm on her skin, making them tingle where he touched. "I'm not your patient," she declared, resisting the urge to shiver.

"Humor me." He looked intently into her eyes. "Tell me where it hurts."

She was caught in the depth of his gaze, the compassion and warmth she saw there causing the butterflies in her belly to flutter. She'd never met anyone like him. He made her want to share her deepest secrets. She'd already told him of her father and helping him in his practice. Now she wanted to finish that story, to tell her most painful emotional wound, and entrust that information to Elliot. But she gave her head a slight shake. Now was not the time. "I hurt everywhere, actually."

Elliot's brow creased. "Let's start with your legs and arms."

Focusing on the here and now, Eden bent down and lifted her left pant leg. The material stuck as she pulled on it, revealing a scrape on her calf. She sucked in a breath. It looked angry, with four long red lines oozing blood. Rolling up her sleeve, she saw another large scrape on her left arm. "The other arm and leg seem fine, just bruised." Her eyes lifted to meet his, but he was staring intently at the wound.

"We need to get those cleaned up." He hunched over to get a closer look at her leg and carefully touched the edges of the wounds. Eden clenched her teeth together to not react to the stab of pain.

Elliot stood and went into the hallway and was back in a flash with a large black bag in his hands. "I think we have everything we need in here." He unzipped the bag and started pulling out first aid supplies. Once they were neatly arranged on the bed beside her, he began to clean the wound. It stung, and tears immediately pricked Eden's eyes, but she didn't let them fall. She thought of the general and the pain he hoped to cause people. Crying made it seem like the general would get his wish somehow, so Eden ground her teeth together and bore the pain with no tears. Thankfully Elliot worked fast, and before long, her leg and arm were both bandaged.

He sat beside her on the bed and gently pressed her arm bandage into place. "Is there anywhere else I should know about?"

She shook her head, and flinched at the movement. "No. Just here." She pointed to the bump near her left temple.

"I have a cold compress for that." He took out a small pouch, like the one he'd given her in the car for her cheek, twisted it firmly, then gave it to her. She carefully placed the compress over the bump and nearly sighed at how good that felt.

"You're a little banged up, but you'll live." Elliot started repacking the first aid supplies. "You could probably use some food and rest, too."

Eden agreed, watching how efficiently he worked getting all the bandages, tape, and compresses put neatly back in their places "I'm sure you could, as well."

He set the bag on the floor. "Definitely." His eyes flicked to the pillow behind her. "You have no idea how tempting it is to find a bed, a couch, or even a little bit of floor to stretch out on and close my eyes." He leaned a little closer and handed her a small, square package. "There were some body wipes in the bag. If you feel anything like I do, I thought you might want to use them to clean up a little bit."

Eden took the package from him, grateful for his thoughtfulness. "Oh, you have no idea. I think the sand and dirt is four layers deep on my skin right now." She gave him a once-over and raised a brow. "If you like, I can share the package with you."

"Is that a hint?" He chuckled. "You don't have to worry, there's a package in there for me and I'll make t-time to use it." He ran a hand over his chin, his gaze flicking to her face. "It's been a long couple of days. We all need a break. Hopefully the general tells us exactly what we want to know so we can go get Amira and p-put this mission behind us."

"If only we can wrap this up that quickly. It would make all our lives so much easier." Eden pulled the compress away and gingerly touched the bump on her head. The bed behind her looked more and more tempting as well. Maybe she could justify a power nap before any new mission orders came in. "Have you heard who is doing the interrogating?"

Elliot leaned back until his shoulders touched the wall, stretching his neck as he did so. "I'm sure it's Luke. He seems to like to have his fingers in all the pies. Most CIA people do."

She lifted an eyebrow and tilted her head. "Oh, really? I had no idea. Is that just a CIA thing?"

He gave her a sidelong glance, his eyes holding a glint of

humor. "With our line of work, I'm sure you have your feelings about intelligence and those who claim to have it."

She gave a low laugh. "Yes, intelligence does seem to be subjective at times. *Especially* in our line of work." Pressing down on the corner of the bandage on her arm, it pulled at the skin and she winced a little.

Elliot straightened, all trace of humor gone. He reached out to touch the bandage edges himself. "Eden, I just want you to know how sorry I am."

"For what?" She looked from the bandage to him, genuinely confused.

He gently took her hand in his and ran his thumb in a slow circle over the back of it. She resisted the urge to suck in her breath. His caress sent warmth shooting up her arm and straight to her middle. How could he evoke such a strong reaction by just holding her hand?

He met her gaze. "For not waiting for backup. For not being more careful. I should have been a better partner and had your back."

Eden went very still. He was apologizing because she'd gotten hurt? Did he think she blamed him somehow?

She turned her hand palm up and intertwined her fingers with his. "Elliot, without your quick thinking and rolling us out of the way of that grenade, I'd have a lot more injuries than some cuts and bruises. You're the reason we're both here. I should be thanking you."

His eyes searched hers, needing reassurance that she was speaking the truth. The moment stretched as unspoken words passed between them with only a look. He lifted her hand and pressed a kiss to her knuckles. "You never have to thank me for that."

For just an instant in a small room in Syria with only one window, the sun's rays shone on them, cutting the darkness that always seemed to follow her. It pushed away the shadows, showing her that there could be light. He lowered their hands, but didn't let go, as if he felt the significance of the moment too. She moved forward, lessening any distance between them. His eyes dipped to her lips. The connection had been there from the start and it only seemed to be getting stronger, binding her to him in a way she couldn't explain. Did she want him to kiss her? Usually, her mind weighed the consequences of any of her decisions within seconds, but right then, all she could think of was him. Them. Right now.

He reached out with his other hand and touched her hair. She leaned into his palm, needing to be closer. "Eden," he started, his voice so quiet she felt more than heard it. But before he could say anything else, Luke came into the room. Elliot's position shielded their hands from view, and they quickly let go of each other.

"How's our patient?" Luke asked, his gaze flicking over them.

Eden cleared her throat and shifted position, moving back farther on the bed. "All bandaged and ready to go," she told him.

"Will your head injury affect your performance in the field?" he asked.

"No. She's got a little b-bump to the head along with some scrapes and bruises," Elliot said, busying himself with the bag at his feet. "Once she has some food in her and some rest, she'll be fine."

"Good to hear. We need every member with us so we can move on Amira the moment we get any intel." Luke took a step back toward the hall. "I'll go see if I can get someone to bring you some soup or something."

"Has the general's interrogation started?" Eden asked. She wanted to be part of that if she could.

"Yes. He's going to be tough to crack, but I think we can do it. The stakes are too high not to." With one last look at both of them, Luke headed out the door, his footsteps receding down the hall.

Eden cleared her throat, suddenly feeling awkward being alone with Elliot. "Looks like we'll be here for a little bit while we wait."

Elliot didn't say anything for a moment, but his eyes never left hers. "Time enough to get some sleep."

"Maybe just a little while we wait for word." She fluffed the pillow and scooted over so she could lie down on her side, but stopped. Did he think she was making room on the bed for him? Her eyes flew to his. "Sleep would be good for you, too. I mean, I'm sure there's another room."

His eyes were keen. His half-smile told her he knew what she'd been thinking. "I'm sure there's another room around here somewhere. For resting. We all need to be at our best for what's coming." His eyes roved over her face and he took a breath like he was going to say something more.

Eden hurriedly cut in. She didn't want to talk about their near-kiss. "Thanks for bandaging me up. It's good to have a doctor so close." She inwardly winced at how that sounded. Of course, he was close. They were sitting closely. And she'd wanted him to be closer. But the moment was gone and now it was just weird.

The edge of his mouth quirked up higher. "I'm glad you like having me close."

Eden could feel her neck flush. He could read her too well. What was it about this man that put all her training at not giving away any emotions by the wayside? Hoping to cover her reaction, she rolled her eyes. "Okay, your bedside manner needs work. Go get some sleep."

He chuckled and stood. "Fine. Before I do, though, I'll make sure your soup is delivered in here and then let everyone know you aren't to be disturbed."

"Unless there's news about the general." Her tone brooked no argument.

"Unless there's news about the general," he agreed with a grin. "Sweet dreams. Call for me if you need anything else."

Once he was gone, she settled down on her side and pulled the pillow to her, confused, but feeling lighter than she had in years. She smiled to herself. Elliot was so easy to have around. He had a serious job but liked to laugh. He had empathy and compassion for the well-being of everyone he came in contact with no matter what side they were on. That wasn't the norm in her world where the focus was always on doing whatever it took to accomplish the mission, but she liked it. No matter how much her head warned her to be careful, her heart was giddy for the first time in a very long time. Nothing would come of it, of course, but for just a moment today, she'd been a woman about to be kissed. And she'd liked the thought.

CHAPTER TWELVE

Elliot put one foot in front of the other, heading to the only other bedroom on the first floor. He'd been running on adrenaline for so long, his body had started to crash. Opening the door, he headed straight for the bunk in the corner and laid down. There was no pillow or blanket, but he didn't care. It just felt good to be off his feet.

He stared up at the smoke-stained ceiling, his body not quite ready for sleep yet. Being with Eden and their near-kiss was on a loop in his head. The way the sun had shone on her face, her attempts to stay strong no matter how much pain she was in, her beauty, and their proximity, had all made that moment seem right to bend down and kiss her. She'd looked like she would have welcomed that kiss, too, if Luke hadn't walked in. But maybe the interruption was for the best. If he'd kissed her now, right before they executed a dangerous mission, their focus could be compromised. Feelings for someone on your team could get people killed when you tried to protect them or put their needs first.

He'd been so relieved she hadn't been seriously hurt after the grenade went off, but the scrapes and bump to the head still sent an arrow of guilt through him. He should have known the general would pull something like that. He had no regard for human life and never had. A grenade in a crowded market was a means to an end, a way to help him escape no matter who he hurt. Before bringing Eden here, Elliot had seen to injuries on about a dozen people, but thankfully there had been a clinic nearby for them to receive more treatment. The last time Colt had checked in, no one had died, which was a miracle.

Elliot turned over and sighed. He'd been chasing terrorists for so long. They all felt the same after a while. "The cause" was their only reason for living, and they didn't care about any lives they ruined in the process. The names of the organizations changed, the leaders changed, but they were always focused on recruiting followers and causing as much chaos as possible. Sometimes it felt like Griffin Force was checking off an ever-growing list, chasing the next terrorist that came up the second the last one went down.

It definitely wasn't that way this time. Seeing Atwah's daughter attempt to take her father's place was their chance to stop the suffering before it started. She hadn't yet taken over any leadership position, so they had this window of opportunity to stop her and he didn't want to miss it.

But they had to find her first.

Part of him wanted to be out there, looking for her. Over the last forty-eight hours, though, he'd taken his fair share of lumps, and his body needed to rest, too. He wouldn't be any good to anyone if he was exhausted. He closed his eyes and willed sleep to come. His last thought was of Eden's dark eyes gazing at him as she leaned in, her lips parting slightly as she said his name.

"Elliot. Elliot." Someone was shaking his shoulder. "We need you downstairs right now." Colt's voice was urgent in his ear.

Elliot opened his eyes and it was only his years of training that helped him clear the sleep cobwebs quickly. "What's wrong?" He sat up and swung his legs over the side of the bunk, blinking rapidly and getting his bearings. "What t-time is it?"

"It's early. We have an emergency with General Rakawi."

Elliot ran a hand over his jaw as he stood and followed Colt out the door. They went through a small opening in the kitchen, that led to a set of narrow stone steps. Walking down to the lower level, there was one room with a dirt floor. It must have been used as a vegetable cellar or even a wine cellar at one time. It was small, with only one lightbulb in the center of the ceiling to illuminate it. The general was lying in the middle of the floor holding his chest, struggling to breathe.

Luke was at the general's side, but glanced over at Elliot when they walked in. "Good, you're here." He motioned toward the man on the floor. "We don't know what's wrong. We were just asking questions when he fell over like that." Luke's voice had a thread of anxiety. If anything happened to General Rakawi, their best lead to Amira died with him.

Elliot bent over with his penlight and held the general's eyes open. His pupils were dilated. "Did he eat or drink anything?"

"He asked for a glass of water." Luke pointed to the table where a half-empty glass was sitting. "That's it."

"How long ago?"

Luke shook his head. "I don't know. We came for you the minute he hit the floor. Five minutes tops."

"He must have had a suicide pill on him." Elliot opened the general's mouth, but didn't see anything unusual. He bent down with his ear to his chest, wishing he had his stethoscope. His heartrate and breathing were rapid and there was a faint smell of bitter almonds. Cyanide poisoning. "Colt, he needs an IV right now or we're going to lose him. I need my bag."

Colt moved toward the door, but Eden appeared in the doorway, holding the medical bag. *Perfect timing.* Elliot reached for it. "Thanks. Can you help m-me get this IV in?"

She knelt down beside him and got out the IV supplies. Elliot rummaged through the bag, hoping they had the antidote that could reverse the poisoning. It took a minute, but with a sigh of relief, he found what he needed. Eden extended the general's arm, put on the tourniquet, and began looking for veins near the bend in his elbow. She moved aside, so Elliot could get closer. "He has a good vein right here."

They worked together to get the IV inserted and the antidote flowing through him. Elliot monitored the general's heartrate closely, hoping for improvement, when he started gasping and choking. They immediately rolled him to his side. The general vomited on the floor, mostly liquid and foam. When he was through, they carefully moved him away from the mess. Colt kicked dirt over the vomit, while the rest of them in the room seemed to collectively hold their breath until the general slowly began to speak, his voice barely more than a croak.

"Let me die," General Rakawi pleaded.

"Tell us what you know," Elliot leaned close to his ear. "A

clear conscience will help your transition to the afterworld when it's your t-time."

The general coughed slightly and closed his eyes. "I know nothing."

"Where is the meeting for the Council of Seven?" Luke asked, kneeling on the general's other side. "And when is it?"

"I know nothing," he whispered.

"Let's sit him up." Luke walked around behind the general, bending to take his arm.

General Rakawi was not a small man. His broad shoulders and wide girth made it difficult to even prop him against the wall. He slouched down and his head lolled to one side. Elliot made sure the IV line was clear in his new position.

"If you help us, we can relocate you," Luke promised. "No one will ever know of our conversation."

The general snorted in amusement and his heavy brows lowered as if he were irritated such a silly thing had even been proposed. "There are eyes and ears everywhere. Spies and traitors report everything. No one is safe."

"I'm surprised Amira was able to recruit you to her cause," Elliot put in. It was the one thing that had been bothering him about Amira's involvement. "She's a woman with no experience in the ways of war."

"She's Atwah's daughter, she's lived through war. She has experience." The general sat up straighter and clenched his fists. "Her father showed her his plans, told her of his vision for the caliphate. And she fought alongside him until his murder." His breathing accelerated again and he spit on the ground beside him. "He was murdered by the West for merely wanting a better world."

"He was murdered by Amira's own order. I was there." Elliot leaned against the doorway, his gaze watchful. The conversation had upset the general which was surprising. Usually, the man was like a brick wall, with no reaction to anything that was said.

"You lie. Amira would never hurt her father. She loved him. Honored him." The general turned his head away and coughed into his hand.

Elliot shook his head. Amira apparently had a loving daughter image going on that was as far from the truth as it could be. "She wanted his fingerprints, and once she had them, she ordered her guard to shoot him. And he did. I'm sure once the rubble is cleared from the underground hospital in Idlib, his body will be found and you will remember this moment. I'm telling the truth." Elliot motioned toward Eden. "She was there, too. A s-second witness."

Eden stared down at the general, but he turned away and wouldn't meet her gaze. "Everything he's saying is true." She moved forward and crouched down so she was eye-level with the general. "Amira wants to take over for her father, but she can't do it without you and the others who escaped. She's only using you."

General Rakawai sniffed. "Of course she needs those who can help win the war, to help realize the dream of the caliphate. Amira is her father's daughter and we will help her to honor his memory." The general's eyes closed, the dark circles under them more pronounced. "It is not unusual for a woman of her strength and vision to want to lead the people. She was born to lead."

"Men are supposed to lead the women and children," Luke supplied. "You know that."

General Rakawi opened his eyes and speared them all with a hard glance. "There is a legend of a woman who can unite the people. Amira will be that woman. It is plain to see."

"So, you're helping her gain a position on the Council of Seven to unite all those who want a caliphate?" Eden asked. She leaned closer. "Why not take that position yourself? You have the military experience and the strength and vision you talked about Amira having."

The general shook his head slowly from side to side. "You don't understand. Amira can unite us all. She is the only one who can offer that."

Elliot could hardly believe what he was hearing. "How?" It was well-known that General Rakawi had no use for women. He dismissed them as easily as he would an annoying servant.

"I'm sure you will find out." The general slumped down once again. "Very soon."

"What if we reunited you with your wife and children and took you somewhere safe?" Luke asked. "Would that be worth something to you?"

He raised his head. "My wife? I have not spoken to her in many years. My children have grown up without me. No," he said gruffly. "Seeing so many united to our cause and witnessing the defeat of the West is all that I have. There is nothing you can promise me."

"What if we could prove that Amira killed her father? Would that change your m-mind about helping her?" Elliot asked.

"Perhaps." He lifted a shoulder. "But you will not have time to do that." His eyes had a light in them and his lips twisted into a sneer, as if he enjoyed the cat-and-mouse game he was playing.

"Well, then, if there's nothing we can offer you and we're running out of time, I think we'll just send you to a blacksite to serve out the rest of your sentence." Luke leaned in, his nose nearly touching the general's. "And forget all about you."

The general stared back, his jaw set, as if he'd known all along it would come to this. "Do as you please. It makes no difference."

Luke stood, his arms folded across his chest. Colt entered the room and went straight to Luke. He spoke softly, but his words could still be heard, as if he wanted the general to hear. "We picked up the finance officer and Atwah's uncle, Asem. It shouldn't be long now before we have Amira in custody."

Luke unfolded his arms and let out a breath. "Excellent." He looked down at the general. "I guess we don't need you after all." He took the three steps to the doorway, where Elliot was standing. "Check him over for any other medication. I'll post a guard outside the door until he's ready for transport."

Elliot nodded and moved to the general. He still wore the colorful shirt he'd stolen from the *souk*, but it was large and ill-fitting. The loose folds of both his shirt and pants created a lot of room for hiding places. Elliot made him stand up and he patted him down slowly, trying to feel for anything out of the ordinary. There wasn't anything on his person, but Elliot noticed a bit of faded writing on the inside of Rakawi's wrist. They both stared at the mark for a moment, then Elliot lifted his head to look into the general's eyes. There was a flicker of fear there before he could mask it. Unsure what it meant, Elliot held the general's wrist firmly with one hand and took out his phone with the other to snap a picture. As soon as he was done the general snatched his hand away and stepped back, rubbing the markings away.

Eden watched the general, her eyes unreadable. "Did you ever have a conscience?"

Rakawi tilted his head to the ceiling for a moment, an air of condescension wrapping around him as he looked at Eden. "A conscience is for the weak," he told her brusquely, as if she were a naïve girl who didn't deserve his notice.

Eden shook her head and pulled herself up to her full height. "I pity you."

Once Elliot was done, the general slumped down into a chair at the table, and Eden and Elliot stepped into the hall. The guard was in place as Luke had promised.

Elliot stopped Eden before she could go upstairs, showing her the picture he'd taken. "The general had some letters and numbers on his wrist. Looks like some kind of c-code."

Eden's brows lowered as she zoomed in on the faded writing. "It could be nothing. Maybe something he had from the prison. It's pretty faded."

"But it could be something. It's still clear enough to be read, so I don't think it's b-been there long. And the general wasn't happy I'd found it. It could be some sort of c-code for where the meeting place is." Elliot looked over her shoulder at the picture. "Maybe in all the excitement today, he forgot to rub it off."

She stared at the random numbers and letters. "Okay, if we think it's a code, we'll break it and see what we come up with."

"Not a problem at all," Elliot teased, unable to resist. "Let me go get my top-secret code-breaking book and I'll be able to t-tell you what it means before you can say Elliot Burke."

She huffed out a laugh. "Leave it to me. I've actually done some code-breaking." She was completely focused on the picture, biting her lip as she peered at it. "I need to get a pencil and paper for notes."

Elliot stared down at the woman in front of him. She was full of surprises---and he liked that about her. "Let's go get you what you need."

She grinned up at him, a genuine happy smile that made his heart skip a beat. "Once I've figured this out, we'll grab Amira and save the world."

"Again." He gave a low chuckle and quirked a brow. "I mean, I know I've saved it a f-few times. I'm only assuming you have, too."

"Oh definitely. A few times. Probably more than you." Her smile widened and she nudged his shoulder as they headed upstairs. Maybe all wasn't lost after all.

CHAPTER THIRTEEN

Even though she'd only managed to grab a few hours of sleep earlier, Eden felt refreshed and ready to go. She pulled out a rickety-looking wooden chair and sat at the small table in the corner of the living room, clutching Elliot's phone with the picture of the numbers and letters on General Rakawi's wrist. The letters and numbers were written in black ink, a small scrawl just below his palm. Some were more faded than others, making it seem as if they had come off due to sweat or possibly rubbing his hands together. It definitely could be a code.

It didn't take long for Elliot to join her. "Were you able to get much sleep?"

"Probably about as much as you did." She laid the phone on the table between them. "Al-Qaeda generally uses the 10-code system. This looks like it could be that."

"Wasn't that just for phone numbers, though? This code has letters and looks different." Elliot peered down at the picture.

"Let's see what we've got." Eden took her own piece of paper and a pencil and began to work through the letters and numbers with the 10-code key to see what she came up with. It didn't take long to see that Elliot was right, it wasn't exactly 10-code. "When I write it all out using the code key, if I vary it just a bit," she tilted her head, her gaze on her notes. "Those look like coordinates to me."

"Coordinates to the C-council of Seven meeting?" Elliot's voice held a thread of hope. "Could it be that easy?"

Luke walked in behind them, skirting around the low furniture with brightly colored cushions on them. "Find something?" He moved a bit faster when he saw them looking at a phone. "A lead?"

"Maybe." Eden showed him her notes, not sure if they would make sense to anyone but her. "Elliot found some writing on the inside of the general's wrist. We think it was written in a variation of al-Qaeda's 10-code. It could be coordinates."

"But you're not sure what it is, or if it has anything to do with the meeting or Amira." A flicker of disappointment crossed Luke's face before he inhaled and leaned down. "Let's take a look at what those coordinates could be." He grabbed his laptop bag off the floor and unzipped it. Pulling the laptop out, he sat down on another rickety wooden chair that groaned under Luke's weight. The man didn't have an ounce of fat on him, but the chairs looked like they'd been made for delicate old ladies to take tea on.

Luke balanced the laptop on his knees, punching in some keys. After a few moments, he looked over his screen. "If they are coordinates, they lead to somewhere on the outskirts of

Idlib. Would they hold their meeting so close to town? Or is it just another safehouse?"

"That part of t-town is known as an ISIS stronghold. They'd feel safe there." Elliot moved closer to look at the computer screen. "If we could confirm this . . ." his voice trailed off, but Eden knew exactly what he was thinking. It would be the chance of a lifetime to get a location and possibly take down seven heads of the most wanted terrorist organizations in the region, if not the world.

She couldn't help the thrill of excitement that went through her at the thought. Thousands of lives could be saved. Not only those who would be targets, but those young men who'd been deceived and blindly followed radical leaders who didn't care one whit about them. Her brother's face swam before her eyes. As the older sister, she should have known what was going on with Ben and protected him. But she'd failed, and he'd paid the price. She pushed her emotions away. It wouldn't do any good to think of Ben now. She had to focus.

"Getting close to them is a pretty big *if*, though." Luke shook his head in frustration. "It just seems too easy. Why would the general carry coordinates on him? This could be just another way to throw us off the real location like Amira did earlier."

"Or the general got careless. He's been in prison a while, not used to being on the run. Maybe he forgot about the coordinates when he got cornered and caught? He was the only one who had to use a secondary exfil site." Eden folded her arms. She didn't want Luke to dismiss the thought that the meeting was exactly where those coordinates pointed. "And if Amira was looking for a specific skillset, at one time, General Rakawi was the head of security in Atwah's organization. Maybe he was supposed to meet Amira there and provide security for her. I mean, we have to at least consider it."

"We'll consider every angle," Luke assured her. "But those angles we're considering also include that this is just another distraction."

"Any news on Amira or the others?" Eden changed the subject, wishing they had something more to go on besides a hunch on coordinates. She hated that they were grasping at straws with so much on the line.

"No. We had several leads, but they're gone. It's like every last one of them vanished into thin air. Again." Luke pushed a frustrated sigh through his mouth. "There are so many hiding places and people who help them. It's like trying to catch a leaf in a hurricane."

Which was why it was so aggravating that they'd escaped. Multiple agencies had worked long hours to capture them in the first place. "So, we'll look at the coordinates, make a judgment on whether they're legit or not, and go from there then?" Eden didn't really expect an answer to her question, but they were running out of options. And time.

"I'll go check in with Isaac." Luke took one last look at the laptop before he left.

Eden's shoulders sagged as she stared at the laptop. Was it all a fraud? A distraction like Luke thought? She needed to hear Elliot's opinion and get out of her own head. "What does your gut tell you?"

"That the general got careless or was arrogant enough to think he wouldn't get c-caught. I don't think these are some random coordinates." Elliot took the chair next to hers, which Luke had vacated. "I'm sure they'll send a t-team to check it out. They have to."

"I want to be on that team." She shifted in her chair and turned toward him. "We're all thinking the same thing. If we do this, we could get a location on and maybe take down seven terrorist heads in this region including al-Qaeda, ISIS, HTS, Hezbollah, Atwah's group, al-Rahman Legion, and Hurras al-Din. We'd get a little bit of peace. I mean, of course others would replace them, but we'd deal every one of their organizations a pretty big blow." Beyond what had happened with her brother, Eden couldn't imagine having so many terrorist organizations thrown into a leaderless chaos. It would definitely put a pause on whatever attacks they had planned. She wouldn't mind witnessing that and being part of it. Getting some justice for what they'd done to her family and thousands of others.

"It's like cutting off the head of the hydra, sometimes. More heads always appear, b-but you're right, it would be huge." Elliot ran a hand through his hair. "It's pretty risky to m-meet for that reason alone. They have to know that."

"Maybe some of them are calling in, but we could get a lock on their location. If they do show, you know security will be incredibly tight, and they'll have more than one escape route planned." Eden looked over at the coordinates again, her mind going over all the possibilities. "On the outskirts of the city, they probably have tunnels."

Elliot grimaced. "I've had my fill of tunnels. They are not my friend."

"Mine, either, actually, but it's their route of choice these days." She gingerly touched her cheek. The skin felt tight from the cut.

"Is the pain worse?" Elliot asked quietly. "You d-don't have to hide it from me, you know."

His concern warmed her all the way to her toes. "I'm fine." How long had it been since she'd had someone worried over her and not whether she could complete the mission or not?

"Do you need an ibuprofen? Or something stronger?" He leaned toward her slightly, and she was reminded of their near-kiss not many hours before. What would he do if she pulled his face to hers and kissed him right now? She quickly glanced around the room, at the team members filing into the kitchen. No one was paying attention to them at the moment, but a kiss would draw their eyes. It would be unprofessional and put everyone in an awkward position. She couldn't---wouldn't---do that, but Elliot tempted her like no one else ever had.

Pulling her mind back to the conversation at hand, she gave a slight shake of her head. "No meds. I'm good." She wanted to feel it all---the pain from the battle wounds, and hopefully, the exhilaration of victory.

"It's more than a little cut. You took a pretty g-good punch. No shame in taking something to help deal with an injury. Nothing that will d-dull your senses, only dull the pain. Take the edge off."

He was so earnest, she pressed her lips together to keep from smiling. "No, thank you. I'll be fine. Don't worry about me." Though it did feel nice for a moment to have him worry just a little about her.

He wouldn't let it go. "What about your scrapes? Are those feeling okay?"

"Yes, doctor," she said, exasperation creeping into her tone. "You know, I do have medical experience myself," she added.

"A doctor or nurse is their own worst patient," he told her, a twinkle in his eye. "It's my j-job to check up on you."

"I'll let you know if I need anything," she said, scooting her chair back so she could stand up. "Let's go see what Luke found out." She needed a little distance from Elliot before she did something she might regret later.

They went into the kitchen area, where the table had been turned into a sort of war room. Laptops and papers were strewn about, as well as maps. Colt, Jake, Nate, Brenna, Abby, and Augie crowded around it with Luke, David, and Isaac. They were on opposite sides of the table, talking about the same thing. Eden went to stand by David and wasn't surprised that Elliot went to Colt, though it was starting to feel strange not having him at her side.

"Easy leads have been proven to be a diversion tactic for the true mission," David was saying. "I don't think those are the coordinates for the meeting. A safehouse, perhaps."

Eden shook her head, not hesitating to jump in. "I think the general got caught trying to escape and didn't get rid of the evidence like he planned to. Why would he need coordinates to his own safehouse? They have to be for the meeting and he was going there to provide security for Amira. It's the only explanation that makes sense to me."

"But if they aren't the coordinates, we're left with Amira gaining a place at the table while we look ridiculous for having fallen for all her ploys." David turned to face her, his expression closed and his arms folded. "I hate looking ridiculous. We're trained agents. Surely we can find a way to confirm what you suspect or find some sort of solid lead before we go chasing our tails."

Eden held up a hand. "No one wants to look ridiculous, but we don't have time for confirmation or chasing leads. We have access to some of the best intelligence agents in the world and even they haven't been able to help us get a lead on Amira's whereabouts." She put a hand on David's shoulder. "This could be a ploy, but I don't think it is. The general has been in prison for over two years. He got careless."

Augie moved to stand next to Eden. "Hi, I'm Augie, nice to meet you." He stuck out his hand and Eden quickly shook it. "I think you're right about the coordinates and this is our best lead at the moment. There's no chatter, not even a whisper of this meeting anywhere online. But I did find out that the al-Qaeda's number two guy is going to be coordinating some of their upcoming 'war effort.' Why would he need to take over unless their leader is going to be busy at this meeting?"

Jake had stood silently, his focus on the map as the rest of them talked, but before Augie even finished, he nodded in agreement. "I think we should treat those coordinates as if this is where the council meeting will be held." He looked over at Colt. "We'll plan the mission as if it is. If we're successful, we'll have the opportunity for the biggest captures in the history of the war on terror."

"And if we don't, we'll have the biggest egg on our faces," David muttered.

Augie took a breath as if to say something more, but then pressed his lips together. It was a good decision. In Eden's experience, when David was set in his opinion, not much changed it. But she knew he was wrong this time. No one else said anything, not even Luke or Isaac. "What do you think, Isaac?"

Isaac's chin hit his chest and he folded his arms, taking a moment before he spoke. They all waited until he lifted his eyes and looked around the table. "I have a contact who tells me they have details about Amira's deal and where the exchange will be to get the four mid-range missiles. I plan to follow up on that. If our team goes to surveil the house, and I go to the possible arms deal, we'll have two chances to find Amira and bring her in."

"What kind of source?" Luke asked, turning to face Isaac fully. "One you can trust?"

"One I've used before." He patted Luke's back. "Do not worry. I'll leave as soon as we're done here and be back in a day or two, hopefully with the confirmation we need of Amira's whereabouts."

"I like that plan, a two-prong approach can cast a wider net for her," Colt told Isaac. "But be careful. Loyalties seem to be shifting more rapidly than the dust under our feet." He moved closer to the table and put his finger on the map. "The coordinates lead to a two-story house in the middle of a street." He pointed at the spot highlighted on the map. "Nothing significant about the house or the neighborhood."

"Probably t-tunnels," Elliot put in with a half-groan, and Eden held back a smile. He really was done with underground tunnels. So was she, if she was being honest. The tight spaces and constant threat of a cave-in or even a gunman waiting underground added another level of stress to an already stressful situation.

"Tunnels are a given," Jake said. "The street-facing side

doesn't have a lot of cover positions for us. It will be easy for them to spot any movement. The back is an alley. More cover, but in a tight space."

"Probably why they picked that l-location." Elliot looked over Colt's shoulder. "Easy to guard, known location, and tunnels."

That gave Eden an idea. "Maybe the tunnels are where we wait for whoever shows up. If they see us above ground, they'll head for the escape route, and that's where we'll be waiting. A nice little trap."

Jake glanced over at her. "I like it. Now we need to figure out where the tunnel entrances and exits are and decide who's going down there to wait for the prize."

Eden dipped her chin. Everyone knew she wanted to be on that team, but the best operatives for the mission would be chosen and she would accept whatever decision was made.

"It'll be tough scoping out the target without being seen." Augie glanced around to each person in the room. "They'll have twenty-four-hour surveillance, cameras and drones. They'll know every movement in the area." He gestured to Abby, Brenna, and the computer techs from Chol behind him. "Between all of us, I think there's a chance we can hack their system and help conceal you long enough to get what you need. And if they're doing a video call, we can hopefully pinpoint each leader's exact location. If we're lucky, we can have teams ready to move in."

"Another day on the job," Jake told him, stroking his beard. "We'll blend in like we always do. Easy day."

Everyone chuckled, and that broke the tension a bit. Eden let the smile fade from her face and slowly exhaled. This mission was a huge opportunity that could make a difference in the world as they knew it. It needed to be well-executed. She looked across at everyone on Griffin Force. She was confident in her team, but there was an extra bit of reassurance to have Griffin Force with them. They had a reputation for being quick and thorough, both qualities they needed for success.

And she hoped they were as good as she'd heard they were.

CHAPTER FOURTEEN

Elliot was surprised Luke had been able to find an upper story apartment miraculously available across the street and halfway down the block from the place where they believed the Council of Seven were meeting. Hopefully whoever currently lived there had been compensated well for its use. The apartment featured a balcony with a great angle for observing any comings and goings on the target house, but wasn't immediately in anyone's line of sight that might be watching for them.

They quickly figured out assignments for surveillance and sleeping. Usually stakeouts weren't that exciting, but having Eden there changed everything. She'd stood by him at the first briefing, her arm brushing his, but she never seemed to lose focus at the contact like he did. They were given the first rotation of surveillance. It didn't take long to set up on the balcony, making sure their position wouldn't be compromised. Augie and Abby were trying to get satellite overwatch up and running, but it was slow going. Elliot settled in with his binoculars, while Eden set up beside him with a camera. After half an hour with no movement detected, Elliot yawned and gave Eden a side glance.

"Do you think this is the p-place?" he asked her. If it was, they should be seeing movement by now.

"Absolutely." She stretched her arms over her head, carefully twisting her neck from side to side. "How are you feeling?"

"Tired and sore. How's your cheek?" Most people he treated gave him little clues as to how they were really feeling. Eden didn't.

"Sore. What a pair we are." She let out a low chuckle.

"Wounded warriors that are still in the fight." He shifted a little closer to her. He loved her laugh.

She sobered. "We could change the face of the war on terror if we can capture even one of the Council of Seven."

"Do you think they'll be here personally or virtually? I'm hoping in person, of course, b-but if Augie gets everything set up with the satellite, we can at least get a l-location if they're virtual." Elliot hoped he could, anyway. Everything seemed a little more difficult in this part of the world. Eden didn't answer him and he wondered what was going on in her head. Her eyes had a faraway look in them. Was she thinking about her family? "Will you find peace for your family's death if this mission is a success?"

She met his gaze, her deep brown depths unreadable. "This war has taken so many lives. I want peace for myself---and the world."

He reached out and squeezed her hand. "If anyone can get us there, you c-can. You've made a difference in the world already and I know your family would be proud." She squeezed his hand back, but didn't draw away. Her fingers felt good in his---right. "If the war on t-terror was ever over, what would you do?"

She thought for a moment. "Probably be a nurse. I have so many good memories of my mom and dad and helping to heal people with them. It's in my blood I think." A small smile played on her lips. "What about you?"

"Same. Healing people and helping p-people. That's all I've ever wanted to do." The connection and familiarity he'd felt from the moment he'd met her waxed stronger. "I think we've been walking similar paths."

"Yes, we have." Her eyes were bright and Elliot inched closer to her.

The balcony door opened and Nate walked out. Elliot quickly drew back, dropping Eden's hand. He didn't miss Nate's raised eyebrows and Elliot tilted his head. Was he going to say something?

"Any updates?" was all Nate said.

"No. Nothing to report." Elliot took the binoculars off from around his neck.

"Okay. Jake and I will take over while you guys go get something to eat." He held out his hand for the binoculars, but Elliot didn't hand them over.

"How's your head? Feeling any c-concussion symptoms?" Elliot looked closer. Nate seemed to be back to his old self, but concussions weren't anything to mess around with.

"No dizziness, no pain. I think I'm good." Nate went ahead and took the binoculars from him. "Don't worry. You'll be the first person I call if I need something."

"Okay. Don't make me regret g-giving you clearance to be here." Elliot gave him a stern look and Nate snorted a laugh and mock-saluted.

Elliot smiled and shook his head before he followed Eden back into the house. Colt and Luke were hashing out possible entrances and exits to the tunnel and whether drone surveillance was a possibility at all. Elliot sat in a kitchen chair in the corner, watching them go back and forth. Eden went to the refrigerator.

"We need to put a small team together and do some up close reconnaissance," Colt said, pointing to a spot on the map in front of them. "We've got to see what we're up against first hand."

"We'd have to be invisible." Luke's tone was firm. "If anyone even gets a whiff that their meeting place is compromised, the whole thing'll be canceled and moved somewhere else in a heartbeat."

"My team can blend in. We can move out in an hour." Colt trained them hard and he was right to have confidence in Griffin Force. They could handle it.

Eden was at the counter, making herself a sandwich with some thick black bread. She glanced up at the conversation happening near the table every now and then, but seemed focused on her food. Elliot's mouth began to water and he realized he couldn't recall eating anything for lunch or much for breakfast.

He stood and walked over to her. "Is there enough for two sandwiches?" He kept his voice low so as to not interrupt Luke and Colt.

She nodded, but didn't say anything, just slid the bread,

meat, and cheese over to him. There was some sort of pesto in a small bowl, and Elliot quickly put together a sandwich for himself. Biting into it, he was surprised at how good it tasted. There was a spice in the pesto that he'd never had before that added an unexpected zing. He took his time and enjoyed the rest of the sandwich, getting something in his stomach helping to calm his thoughts. They could do this. Blending. Executing a mission. Griffin Force had done this hundreds of times when stakes were high. They could do it again. Colt and Luke were wrapping up, which meant the team would be headed out soon.

"What do you think of the p-plan so far?" he asked Eden. She'd finished her sandwich, her eyes on the men at the table.

She delicately brushed the crumbs from her fingers. "Seems like a good plan to me with the intel we currently have. We have to make sure we're at the right place, and if we are, I definitely want to be on the tunnel team."

That didn't surprise him. She liked being in the thick of the action. "Wouldn't it be more f-fun above ground, making them run for the tunnels?" He was trying to keep it light, but his protective instincts were kicking in. He wanted her as safe as possible and being above ground was definitely safer than the tunnels.

"Fun, yes, but I want to see the look on their faces when they realize they're trapped. That they aren't as smart as they think they are." Her voice had a bitter edge to it, one he'd never heard from her before.

He leaned against the counter and caught her gaze. "Which one are you looking f-forward to capturing the most?" But he knew the answer before he'd even asked the question. He'd seen her reaction to Atwah in the hospital tunnel. It was definitely him.

"I would have loved to capture Atwah." She let out a long breath and shrugged her shoulders. "Since he's dead, I want to make sure his daughter doesn't have a chance to take over for him. So many lives have already been destroyed because of his foolish 'cause.'" She looked away, but didn't hesitate when she said it.

"He's the one that killed your father," Elliot guessed. She held very still, her breathing shallow. When she turned and her eyes met his, he was shocked at the raw hurt and pain he saw there. It made Elliot want to pull her into his arms. "Eden. I'm sorry for even asking. You d-don't have to t-talk about it if you don't want to."

She sucked in a deep, shaky breath, moving back toward the sink. Elliot moved with her. Whatever she was about to say, she didn't want overheard.

"Atwah took everything I loved away from me." Eden swallowed. "My father and mother were working at a refugee camp on the Israeli/Syrian border when a car full of explosives and two suicide bombers went through. The blast killed them instantly, along with everyone they were treating." She clenched her jaw. "My brother was at university then, and told me he didn't believe it was Atwah's group who'd killed our parents. I should have guessed he was investigating Atwah's cause and was sympathetic toward it. Atwah's recruiters lure in young men and women with pretty words, saying they'll give them a family, give them a purpose to help the greater good, to help oppressed people around the world---and of course not telling them what they're really about until it's too late."

"Is your b-brother still alive?" Elliot asked softly.

She put her arms around herself, as if trying to hold everything in---the pain and the memories. "He left me a voicemail that weekend, telling me of being accepted into an elite freedom fighters' group and that he was going to prove his loyalty. He said I wouldn't understand, but once I did, well, then I'd be proud of him. He was going to change the world. I panicked and did everything I could to find him, but he'd turned off his phone." She hung her head and Elliot leaned forward to hear her voice that was barely more than a whisper. "He died in the explosion at the U.S. Embassy in Jordan."

Elliot froze at her words, time seeming to slow down around him. It all snapped into place. That's why Eden looked so familiar to him. He'd seen her before—well, the man that looked just like her. Elliot had been getting ready to leave that day at the embassy, and he'd seen her brother when he'd approached the gates. He'd been wearing an oversized jacket, his eyes darting back and forth as if looking for a way out. He was a scared kid who didn't really want to die. Elliot and the security guard had talked him down and been so close to helping him take off that suicide vest when something triggered it. The blast was larger than he'd thought it would be, throwing the guard who'd been about five feet in front of him back against a pillar, killing him instantly. Her brother and the guard had died in a horrific way and the entire scene had haunted Elliot for months afterward.

Eden hadn't seemed to notice his reaction. "The security footage showed he was at a side entrance that had a small checkpoint. He was talking to the guard and someone else. I think he must have changed his mind because when he was taking the vest off, it exploded, killing my brother and the security guard." Eden sniffled and closed her eyes, a lone tear escaping down her cheek. "He .. he changed *my* world that day. I lost him and I was alone. Everyone I loved---my entire family---was gone."

Her words were so wrapped up in pain and suffering, Elliot couldn't help pulling her into his arms while they were somewhat shielded from the view of the others at the table. She was motionless, her skin cold to the touch. He gently rubbed her back but didn't say anything, wishing he could absorb some of her heartache. "I'm sorry." Should he tell her he was the one who'd been talking to her brother right before his death?

She pulled away and discreetly wiped her eyes. "I dedicated the rest of my life to trying to capture Atwah and make sure he could never hurt anyone again. And now that he's gone, his daughter wants to take up his cause and keep it going. I can't allow that."

He had to say something, but maybe he needed to wait for the right moment. "I chased Atwah for so long, watching the destruction he left behind and doing what I could to try and help pick up the pieces. It just seems right that we'd both catch a break and not have to start tracking down the next generation."

"Life is never fair. I learned that the hard way." Eden leaned back and glanced at the men in the kitchen who were rolling up the maps. As if she needed something to do with her hands, she grabbed her plate and moved to the sink to rinse it off. "You probably didn't dream of doing this for a job when you were growing up."

He stayed by her side, not too close so she would feel like he was hovering, but he didn't want to let her go too far. Not yet. "No, not this exactly, but I knew I w-wanted to help people. And that's what I do." He reached out and gently touched the skin just below her ear. There was a faint scar there. Was it from her childhood? Or from her time as an operative? She rolled her neck and he dropped his hand. There was so much emotion roiling through her, just below the surface. What could he do for her?

"Would you t-tell me if I could help you?" His heart rate picked up, waiting for her answer, wanting it to be yes. "I'm a pretty good listener."

She met his gaze, her deep brown depths unreadable. "That would depend."

His chest squeezed, knowing he would meet any requirement she gave him. "On what?"

"On whether it was something I could take care of by myself." She lifted her chin without dropping their eye contact, as if she thought he might challenge her in some way.

She was so vulnerable, but at the same time, she was the bravest woman he'd ever met. "Are you afraid to l-let anyone in? To trust that they could help you and b-be there for you?" He leaned forward slightly, his head close to hers.

"Everyone close to me has either been hurt or killed. It changed me." She shrugged a shoulder. "Sometimes it's best just to keep everyone at arms-length. For their own good."

If she was ever going to trust him and let him in, he had to tell her. "Eden, was your b-brother's name Ben?" He knew it was, but he couldn't see any other way to start this conversation.

Her eyebrows drew together. "Yes." She hesitated. "How do you know that?"

Elliot's entire focus was on her, the tension in her shoulders and the wariness on her face sending little darts of pain to his heart, knowing what he said next would be hard for her to hear. "I . . . well, I was there at the embassy that d-day. I was the one t-talking to your b-brother."

Her forehead wrinkled as she stared at him, taking in his face as if she'd never seen him before. "You were the one I saw on the security cameras," she breathed out, her eyes wide. She opened her mouth to say something else, but then stiffened and moved back.

Colt's voice cut in from behind him. "Hey, you two. We're moving out. I'll take Jake, Nate, and David for a little ride through the neighborhood to try to see anything on the ground that we might have missed from our vantage point up here. We found an old beat-up van and we're going to block out the back windows."

Elliot held in a frustrated sigh. Eden's whole demeanor had changed. She was a closed book now. If he had anything to say about it, though, they'd finish this conversation the second they were alone. "Copy that."

Eden turned away and headed toward David. Her posture was stiff and she didn't look back. Was she angry with him? The connection he felt to her was strengthening with every minute he spent with her, but would knowing he was there for her brother's last moments change things between them? From the first time he'd met her it seemed like he'd always known her and he was merely getting to know his best friend again. Those feelings were dangerous with the mission in front of them, but he couldn't help it. He'd thought she'd been feeling it, too, but now he wasn't sure. They needed to finish that conversation.

He headed to the tables where Augie and Abby were working on their computers, cracking his knuckles as he went. He needed to focus and get his head in the game. This was the most important op of his professional life. But somehow, Eden had quickly become an important part of his personal life and he needed to explain what had happened between him and her brother. He didn't want to lose what they had before it even got started.

She was a complication he wanted, but couldn't afford. And he needed to sort it out before the mission went any further.

CHAPTER FIFTEEN

Davidwas talking to her, but she couldn't focus on his words. It was like she was underwater, trying to get to the surface.

Elliot had been with Ben that day.

He'd tried to talk him down and from what she'd seen on the security footage, he'd succeeded, but the vest had gone off prematurely. It was all so unbelievable. What were the chances they would meet like this?

She wanted to finish talking to him, to ask him all the questions that were going through her mind. What had Ben said? What had made him change his mind? Had he talked about his family? Guilt and regret about her brother and how he'd died had run in a painful loop through her heart for so many years she'd just made space for them. But what if there was a chance Elliot had information from that day that would make the pain less fierce? Her brother's last message of wanting her to be proud of him had haunted her. What were his last words before he died? So many questions, but with the team planning to do some recon, there wouldn't be time to get answers.

David paused. "Are you okay?"

Eden didn't trust herself to speak and merely nodded.

"Well, Colt is taking his team out in the van. Augie is hoping they can get some satellite coverage, and I need you back on the balcony overwatch. We have to be aware of any movement at all in or around that house." His posture was stiff, his tone stressed.

"You really think this is one of Amira's distractions again? That it can't possibly be the council's meeting place?" She kept her tone even, not wanting to accuse him.

"She's done it before. Amira has been one step ahead of us this entire mission." He ran his hands through his hair. "If we are here, wasting our energy watching a random house, then she has all the time in the world to escape, to regroup, and to buy those missiles."

"This is the house. I'm sure of it." Eden straightened. "You'll see." She took one last glance at Elliot who was still talking to Colt, then headed toward the balcony overlooking the target area. Slowly walking past Nate, she moved to the far corner position, picked up the scope and held it to her eyes. A perfect view of the front doorway, but she knew no one would use it. Not because this wasn't the right place, but the leaders of the terrorist organizations had stayed alive by being smart and doing the unexpected. Coming through the front doors would be neither of those things. They'd use the tunnels.

As she was putting on her comm headset, Elliot stepped out onto the balcony. He bent and said a few words to Nate. With a nod, Nate got up and went back into the house. Elliot sat down mid-balcony and put on a comm set as well before picking up the binoculars. Her immediate thought was to go to him and finish their conversation, but she couldn't. With their comms on, the team would hear anything said, not to mention that if something was missed on this recon mission, it could blow the whole thing.

Elliot met her gaze. His eyes were full of empathy and compassion, as if he knew her thoughts exactly just as she knew his. They'd have their conversation. He'd make sure of it. The connection between them was still so new to her, but she couldn't deny how strong it felt. She'd confided things in him she hadn't told anyone else and a burden had lifted from her shoulders. He hadn't diminished her feelings or the pain she still struggled with, he'd just held her. It had been a long time since someone had hugged her. The warmth in his embrace had seemed to fill holes in her soul. And now to know he was there for her brother and had tried to save him? That intensified everything she was feeling.

It was all happening in the wrong time and place, though. They were in the middle of a mission. Why couldn't she have met him when this op was over? Or before? She had to have her head in the game, but how he made her feel was a distraction. The only solution was distance, maybe even to take herself off the mission. But there was no way she'd do that. No, she needed to see Amira taken down, to make sure Atwah and his family were done destroying people. Focus was what she needed.

Putting her eye back to her scope, she swept the front entrance again. There hadn't been any unusual activity since they'd gotten here last night and all the inactivity had let her exhaustion creep back in. She needed to rest. Soon. Elliot probably did, too. Her eyes were drawn to him again, as if he was a magnet she couldn't resist. He was watching the street, but must have felt her gaze on him. He glanced her way.

"Any m-movement on the house?"

His simple question meant he must have come to the same conclusion she had. Their conversation about Ben would have to wait. They needed complete front-sight focus on the mission.

"No. All's quiet." She put her eye back to the scope. The sun was rising and people were starting to emerge from their homes. The day was getting started, which meant it was a perfect recon time. The van could disappear in the hustle and bustle of a new day. Idly she wondered with the country in so much chaos, were there many jobs still to go to? The fight for survival was all too real in this part of the world. What had their lives been like before the war?

A woman dressed in a full burqa walked slowly down the street. There was nothing about her that would be suspicious, but the moment she came into Eden's view, the hairs on the back of Eden's neck stood up. "We've got something. Woman approaching target."

Elliot swung his binoculars over to see. "No d-description. Wearing a black burqa."

The woman stopped at the target house and went inside as if she belonged there. "Could be the homeowner," Elliot said quietly, as if just for Eden's ears, but of course anyone on comms could hear.

"You don't believe that. Not when the Council of Seven are meeting there at any time. It could be Amira." It had to be.

"If we could verify that, we'd have the c-confirmation we

need." Elliot looked into his binoculars again, as though the verification was right in front of them, if only they could see it.

"How can we verify that without spooking the rest of the council?" Eden took a slow sweep of the area without her scope. No one else was nearby. Had Colt left with the recon team yet? "If we could just see a face and get facial recognition to confirm it's the people we're looking for."

"That would m-make our job too easy." He gave her a lopsided grin and her heart turned over in her chest. He wasn't like any man she'd met before, keeping things light even in the most stressful situations.

She shook her head. "We can't have that." The job was never easy, but having him close by made it feel less hard.

They shared a smile, then returned to keeping watch on the house. A small black car drove up in front of the target. Two men got out, one of them practically supporting the other and dragging him along. The woman who'd gone in a moment before opened the door, her head bowed so her face wouldn't be shown, and the men quickly went inside---but Eden still caught a glimpse of the man being dragged, his black suit as familiar as his face.

"Did you see that?" Elliot asked, all traces of humor gone.

Eden had pressed her scope so tightly to her eye, there would be a mark, but she had to be sure she was seeing what she'd seen. Her heart was in her throat and she could barely speak. "Yeah." Her voice cracked and she swallowed hard. It couldn't be. There had to be some mistake.

"Was that Isaac? Your b-boss?"

"Yes." He'd been bloody and beaten. Eden's stomach had dropped to her toes when she'd recognized him. How had they gotten to him? What could she do to get him back? Eden started to move away from the edge of the balcony. "I need to talk to David. And Luke." Whatever the plan had been, that all changed with Isaac's capture. They couldn't just leave him to die.

"I'll k-keep an eye on things here," Elliot said. His gaze flicked over her in concern before he turned his attention back to his binoculars.

"Thanks." Eden went back into the room, her movements slow and deliberate. Something was horribly wrong, but there was no need to panic. They could work the problem. She unhooked her earpiece and rolled it over in her hand, turning it off before slipping it into her pants pocket. David and Luke were in the far corner of the room, their heads bent together.

"I'm sure you heard over comms," she said, joining them, trying to think of any plan of action, any move they could make to get him back. "What do we know? Anything?"

"Nothing." Luke's voice was hard. "We have no idea how they would have grabbed him, unless his trusted source gave him up."

Eden sucked in a breath. "Okay. What are we going to do to get him out?"

David looked at her with pity in his eyes. "What can we do? Anything we try will jeopardize the overall mission. We have a chance to grab more than one terrorist leader and save thousands of lives. Or we can save Isaac."

Just hearing the words said aloud made her temper flare. She had to stay calm. With a slight shake of her head, she said, "There has to be something we can do." It couldn't come down to just that. Isaac was like a father to her. She didn't want to lose him.

"Isaac knew the risks of his job." David turned away as if the conversation was over and she grabbed his forearm.

"We can't just leave him to die!" Fear licked through her veins. She'd already lost one father. "Let's ask Griffin Force. Maybe they have some ideas."

David pulled his arm away, his voice hard. "Isaac would be the first one to say let him go. Stick with the mission. You know that."

"No." She looked at Luke. "We can still capture Amira and the others and save him, too. We just have to think it through."

Luke lifted a shoulder. "You know I want that, too. But we're running out of time. If you can think of a plan, let me know and we'll look at all the angles."

Eden ran a hand through her hair. There had to be a way. Security would be tight. The tunnels weren't an option. There was the woman that had entered the house. She'd been wearing a burqa and was obviously known to the man who had Isaac. If she wasn't Amira, she was likely a servant. Maybe Eden could somehow get in as a maid and pass a weapon along to Isaac? Would they use a servant for the meeting to serve the food? She closed her eyes in frustration. They needed more information. Executing a plan without knowing the variables was suicide and David was right, Isaac wouldn't want anyone sacrificing their life for his.

She sat down in the kitchen chair and pulled a blank notepad from the middle of the table toward her. Grabbing the pencil next to it, she began to write down her thoughts, to gather them so she could present a reasonable plan to Luke. She couldn't be emotional. At all. Or this would all be over before it started and Isaac would be dead.

Elliot came in and looked over her shoulder. "Working up a p-plan?"

She nodded. "I think I can get in there." Would he support her? Or was the mission the most important objective?

Elliot abruptly sat down in the chair beside hers. "You're going to g-go in? Alone?"

She tapped the pencil on the notepad. "The woman who went in with a burqa didn't have any trouble. I think I can go in the same way."

"If she's Amira, she wouldn't have any t-trouble. But beyond that, they'll have security and c-code words. You'll be killed on sight if you don't know them." He leaned in and looked over the notes she'd written.

Eden pushed them toward him so he could see her plan. "I think I have a way around that. They're going to use a servant they know, that's a given. Luke has a recording of a previous Council of Seven meeting from his inside source. I'm betting they're going to use the same codes and the same people. I can listen to the recording, familiarize myself with the codes, and then insert myself into one of the female servant's roles. Wearing a burqa would make it easy to be invisible to them."

Elliot was already shaking his head. "That's too risky. They likely change the c-code with each meeting and you won't know that until it's too late."

She leaned forward, wanting him to understand. Needing his support. "I have to try. I can't just leave Isaac to die. You would do the same if this was Colt."

Elliot stared at her for a long moment, then let out a breath. "You're right. I'd do anything for my t-team. How can I help?"

Relief flowed over her at his words. He was going to help her. She wasn't alone.

Eden looked up at the clock on the wall. "I need your help going through the recording as quickly as possible and pulling out any code words. We are really up against the clock."

Elliot pushed back his chair. "Done. I can have Augie help us as well. The m-more eyes we have on this, the better. Did Luke approve the mission?"

She eyed the room where Luke had retreated to oversee the entire op. "Not yet. I was just about to go speak with him."

"Do you want me to c-come with you?" He leaned in close again, and Eden had to resist closing her eyes at his scent. Citrus with a hint of antiseptic all mixed with dust and sweat. It was as sweet-smelling to her as any store-bought aftershave. How could he still smell good with all they'd been through?

"No, I've got this." Though part of her did want him there. It was nice to have backup in some cases. And he never made her feel like she was weak or couldn't handle something. Just that he wanted to help and be her teammate. She liked that.

Squaring her shoulders, she stood and started toward the next room. Luke was on the SAT phone listening to whoever was on the other end, his eyes staring at the gap in the curtains. He turned when he heard her approach. "I'll get back to you," he said, and disconnected the call. "What is it?"

"I think I know how we can get Isaac back." She clasped her hands in front of her, summoning every bit of confidence she had. This was Isaac's only chance and she didn't want to blow it. "I can go in posing as a female servant. We can get the old codes from that recording you have of a previous council meeting, and then I can at least get a weapon to Isaac, if not get him out."

Luke ran a hand over his jaw, but kept his eyes on her face. "That's really risky. I would think they'd change those codes with every meeting."

She lifted her chin. "Perhaps. But they probably use the same people for every meeting, from security to female servants. Why not use the same codes? They would trust the people they'd used before, so it wouldn't be necessary to change the codes when the players were the same. Not to mention, the women generally don't speak at all, or nothing more than a whisper, in most of these men's circles. If I can take the place of a female servant, knowing the previous codes, I think it's doable."

Luke's gaze was penetrating. "If you have any hope of doing this, we need those old codes ASAP. From what I'm hearing we're at the right place and the meeting is going down in the next three hours."

Relief shot through her. He was considering her plan. "I can do it. I just need your okay to at least make an attempt to get him out." She tried to keep any emotion out of her voice, but it was getting harder and harder the more she thought about the odds of getting to Isaac. She squared her shoulders. She could do it. She knew she could.

Luke exhaled sharply. "If I let you do this, it could compromise our mission in stopping Amira or capturing the leaders. And we've only got one chance." He stared at her, his arms folded, his expression hard. "I want to get Isaac back, you know that. But I also want to capture as many terrorist leaders as we can.

She met his gaze head on. "We can do both. We'll have mission success and get Isaac back. I know it. You can trust me."

He was silent for a moment, as if weighing her words. "This is so crazy risky. You realize that if you don't succeed, they'll kill you."

"I know." The thought didn't scare her. She'd be giving her life trying to save another. And hopefully taking down a terrorist or two before she died. That's what she'd known her mission to be the moment her parents were killed and her brother taken from her.

Luke gave her a curt nod. "Okay. Let's get to it, then. We don't have a lot of time."

"Okay." She spun on her heel and went back out to the kitchen area, mission specifics running through her head. Knowing they only had a few hours added a bit of extra pressure. There was so much to do.

Elliot had set up a laptop on the small table they'd been sitting at before and was leaning over Augie's shoulder. "Can you do a search for anything that sounds like a c-code word?" he asked.

Augie bent over to tap something on the keyboard and rewind the recording that was playing. "Yeah. I've been working on a new program to search out voice patterns. Do you know your voice generally raises a bit when you're saying a password?"

Elliot glanced up at Eden and gave her a tight-lipped smile as he spoke. "I had no idea. How accurate is it? We can't afford to m-miss even one."

"You can trust me, El. I've got this." Augie was completely focused on the laptop screen now.

Eden moved to stand next to Elliot. "What's going on?"

He leaned a hip against the table, tilting his head toward

Augie. "We're c-combing through the recording for code words. We were even able to look at the surveillance photos. You were right. The C-council used four female servants for the meeting. All in burqas. And from the recording, they're all whispering. And according to the source, they've used four women several times before for other lower-level meetings." He looked at her and raised his eyebrows. "You might be able to p-pull this off, if you can take one of their places."

"Did you doubt that I could?" She knew he hadn't, but the admiration in his voice and the recognition that she could do this gave her a little ego boost. This idea was going to work. "The big problem now is finding one of the women and replacing her before the meeting."

"With no one else b-being the wiser." Elliot turned back to the computer screen. "I guess you're going to need a burqa."

Most women in Syria wore hijabs, and burqas were pretty common as well. "It won't be hard to get one."

David walked over to them, a frown on his face as he stared at Eden. "I just heard what you're proposing. This is hardly more than a suicide mission."

She didn't have time for David or his negativity. "Do you have a better idea?"

"No. But you'll need backup." He put his hands on his hips and gave her an expectant look.

She shook her head. "There's no way to have back up in there. The only in we have is me posing as a female servant. And you know they'll be checking for wires or any sort of listening devices. The second they see you, they'll run or start shooting. No. I'll be on my own. And I'll be fine."

"Or you'll be dead." David made a snort of disgust. "This

isn't a game, Eden. There are protocols that keep us safe. Not that you've ever followed them like you should."

Eden pinched the bridge of her nose. "I really don't need this right now, David. Leave me be."

"Are you putting on this bravado for the Americans?" he asked, his eyes flashing. "Putting your life at risk to show them how courageous you are?"

"Don't be ridiculous," she snapped. "I'm trying to save Isaac's life and you'd do well to try to help instead of acting like a spoiled child." She turned her back on him. "I have work to do."

She heard him move toward the balcony. It was his turn to watch the scopes in the rotation and maybe that would give him some time to think about what he was really saying. Eden shook her head. He could be such a hothead sometimes, shooting off his mouth when he should be quiet and listen. But he also had flashes of brilliance, using his skills and intelligence that had gotten them out of some tight spots. It was just reining in the anger and curbing his tongue. She'd hoped with more experience that would naturally happen, but he'd been more sullen and reckless lately. Maybe after years of seeing murder and cruelty it was finally getting to him. The powerlessness they all felt when terrorist networks seemed to grow overnight had gotten to more agents than she cared to remember. It affected them all, but field agents more than most.

She sat with Elliot and Augie and got down to work, each of them combing the different parts of the recording and pulling out the code words she might need. She wrote them all down, searing them on her memory. Her life and Isaac's depended on it and she wasn't going to let Isaac down.

Once the entire recording had been gone through, and the last code words written down, Eden rested her head in her hands, her elbows on the table in front of the laptop. Everyone else had gone into the makeshift war room to go over the final plans for the mission. They were almost out of time and she still had so much to do. Closing her eyes, she took a breath. One step at a time. She felt more than heard Elliot approaching her. Her body seemed to be hyper-aware whenever he was near and his presence was comforting. She couldn't explain how. It just was. She looked up to see him standing at her side with a plate of bread and fruit.

"You n-need to keep your strength up," he told her softly.

"Thanks." She didn't take the plate, just watched him, his face so full of concern. His eyes reminded her of her father's sometimes. He'd seen suffering and was one who always wanted to fix it. The tenderness for the human condition was hard to hide, and neither Elliot nor her dad could do it. "What about you?"

"Don't worry about m-me." He took the seat next to her. "Are you sure you're up for this?"

"Are you questioning my abilities, too?" A sliver of disappointment ran through her. She'd truly thought he believed in her and it cut deep to think that he didn't.

"Of course not." He took her hand and squeezed her fingers. "I know you c-can do it. I'm only worried that you've got an emotional connection here. That can c-cloud your judgment. Isaac means a lot to you."

His words hit home. He was saying out loud what she hadn't allowed herself to even think. She let out a little breath. "I know. To be honest, I'm a little afraid of that, too."

He laid a hand gently on her forearm. "Just remember, whatever happens in there, you've got a reason to c-come back alive. You're not alone." His fingers slipped down her arm to her hand, his thumb tracing a circle over the back of it. Tingles ran over her skin at the contact, warmth radiating from his touch straight to her heart.

"Eden." He hesitated a moment, then leaned close. "When all this is over, I'd like to take you somewhere for a nice dinner and c-compare notes on the parts of the world we've seen, things we'd still like to do . . ." his voice trailed off. "And maybe kiss you."

His words rocketed through her. She licked her lips, her heart thundering in her chest. She leaned close, their lips a breath apart. "Why wait?" And then she touched her mouth to his.

He was surprised at first, his kiss tentative, but then one hand stole to the back of her neck and the other cupped her jaw. He scooted closer, then drew her upwards to a standing position and pressed her against him. Her hands went up his chest and circled around his neck, her fingers running through his short hair. He was all muscle and hard lines, his kiss tender, but demanding, just like him. She lost herself in sensation, wanting to stay in this moment forever. When they finally drew apart, their breaths were coming fast and Elliot clasped her in a hug, as if he couldn't bear to let her go yet. They stood there, silent, breathing each other in.

Eden closed her eyes. Why couldn't she have met him sooner? But with their jobs, that would have been impossible. Better to just be grateful for the moments they'd been given. "I have to go," she whispered.

"I know." He kissed her temple. "I'm going to be in the tunnels. If you can get there, I can get you out safely."

"I'll do everything I can." She let her hands slip down his arms, squeezing his fingers before she broke the contact. "I'll see you soon."

And she hoped with every fiber of her being that was true.

CHAPTER SIXTEEN

Elliot watched her go, his heart thumping wildly. How could he have become so attached to her in such a short amount of time? Yet, they'd shared so much since the moment they'd met. A crucible of sorts that had bonded them together in ways he couldn't have imagined. He wanted to call her back, to hear her laugh one more time, to kiss her until she would never forget him. But there was a mission that needed her more than he did.

He turned back to the table and sat down. They'd done everything they could to ensure her safety. Now he needed to hold up his end of the bargain and be in a position to help her if she managed to make it down to the tunnels. It was going to be tricky to stay hidden, as it was most likely the tunnels would be the entrance and exit for the entire council. But that was his job---to stay invisible.

Colt walked into the room, following by Nate and Jake. "With Isaac's arrival, the recon mission is scrubbed. We know this is the place and we need to keep that information quiet so someone wanting to take out the competition doesn't get trigger happy and bomb the whole place to kingdom come. We're putting our original plan into action. Time to get in position and surprise them in the tunnels."

"How are things looking?" Elliot asked. This mission had a lot of risks to it and they couldn't plan for everything.

Colt gave him a half-smile. "About the same as always."

"That b-bad?"

"Yup. But we've been here before. We'll make it work. Security is tight around the entrance to the tunnel, but we think we've found another way in. Augie's been mapping where the tunnels might start and end. He was trying to explain how he had combined Lidar images with satellite photographs, but I didn't really understand exactly what he was talking about." He grinned and shook his head. "But the point is, he found another way in. It'll take some work, though." Colt passed Elliot his gear.

Work was just what Elliot needed to keep his mind off Eden. "What k-kind of work?"

"We can't get through the guards without giving away our position, so we're going to punch through our own entrance. Which means we've got to dig." Colt slapped him on the shoulder. "Remember that mission in Afghanistan?"

Elliot groaned. "It took my arms a week to recover from that op. We practically d-dug a new tunnel."

"Pazir never knew what hit him, though, when our tunnel finally met up with his. And we stopped a minor arms dealer from becoming a major player." Colt stopped and gave him a look. "El, I have to ask. Is your head going to be where it needs to be? I can't have anyone on the team thinking about anything else besides this mission."

Did he know about Eden? He ran a hand over his jaw. Had Colt seen something? "What do you m-mean?"

"I see how you look at her, man. I get it. But we need you focused up." Colt raised his eyebrows. "We good?"

"We're g-good." And he would be. He wanted this mission to be successful and for all of them to make it out alive. To do that, they all had to work together as a team. Focused-up, like Colt said. "Have you heard how they're g-going to replace one of the women with Eden?"

"The vehicle bringing the women here just had a little accident. There were witnesses, so the driver had no choice but to take them to a clinic for treatment. Luke had people there waiting and Eden should be taking one of the women's places right now." He picked up his vest. "Everything's going according to plan."

Hopefully it was a seamless switch for Eden. And no one noticed anything different about her.

Colt shifted over to the table where the gear was laid out. "Augie says that some cryptic chatter he's been monitoring suggests that the meeting starts in less than two hours, so we've got to make our entrance, then get in position. Time for the team to tac up and let's get out of here."

Elliot nodded and started getting ready. It didn't take long to kit up and they were leaving the house by the back way, careful not to be seen. Security forces were starting to get noticeable around the target house, probably a few for each leader, and they'd set up a perimeter with checkpoints. No one was getting through. The streets that had been teeming with people just starting their day not more than an hour ago were now empty---as if the entire neighborhood was holding its breath like it knew something was about to go down. Despite all that, Luke and his team had found a home that was on the outer edge of the perimeter where security wasn't as tight. And if Augie's calculations were correct, the house was right on top of a far corner of the tunnel. That's where they would dig.

They kept to the alleys and shadows until they made it to the empty home. Colt went in first and the rest of the team followed, not speaking, using only hand signals. If they were spotted now the entire mission would be tanked and Isaac and Eden would most likely be killed. They had to stay invisible.

Luke took over and led them all to a small spot in the kitchen. He marked an X in the dirt and Colt got out his entrenching tool, which was more or less a folding shovel with a serrated edge. There was also one that unfolded into a pick-axe. Colt motioned for Jake and they started digging through the floor. Nate and Elliot used two buckets they'd found near the home's kitchen sink to keep the dirt clear, while Luke kept watch. They rotated through every twenty minutes to keep as fresh as possible. Elliot was also keeping a close eye on the time, knowing their window was closing. They had to be in position before the meeting started.

An extra thread of anxiety wound around his gut. This mission would have so many repercussions if they could pull it off. And so many consequences if they couldn't. There was no room for error. He pushed his shovel in a little harder, wishing they were already punching through. How deep did they have to go?

Colt motioned him to rotate and he pushed himself up to

take a position at the window. They had to get this done faster somehow. He peered out the window and saw movement out of the corner of his eye. He immediately signaled for everyone's silence. Elliot leaned against the wall, flattening himself as much as possible, while still keeping an eye on what was coming. It was a patrol team. Four guys going house to house. Elliot signaled four and Colt quietly began covering the hole in the floor with a rug. The digging team retreated into the next room. The patrol drew closer, looking in windows, but not entering any of the houses. That could work in their favor if they didn't see anything amiss.

They turned toward Elliot and he sank down, his fingers closing around his combat knife. Using a gun would be the last resort if anything happened. A gunshot would bring everyone running. He listened as the men in the patrol grumbled about their assignment. They were only doing cursory checks, anxious to get back to their stations where food was awaiting them. Who knew a hungry patrol team was what would keep Griffin Force from being discovered? They checked in the window right above him, but quickly moved away. Elliot straightened, watching them until they were out of sight.

"All clear," he said softly. Colt, Jake, and Luke all came back into the room. Nate nodded to him from the window on the other side. "We've got to m-move this along," he told them. "We're running out of t-time."

Colt nodded and they all took up their positions again, the shovels moving faster than they had before---until one of them clanged. Elliot's stomach dropped. That sound could mean only one thing. They'd hit stone. *No, no, no.* They didn't have time for this. He looked over at Colt who was staring down into the hole they'd made. Elliot wanted to leave his post and ask what was going on, but he held steady. Colt began digging again, about four inches further away than he had been. Elliot let out a sigh of relief. There was a way around it.

Jake stood and came over to take Elliot's place at the window. "Don't worry. We've got this." He grinned and patted Elliot's shoulder as they switched positions.

"Easy day," Elliot said as he moved toward the hole. They were going to punch through right now if Elliot had anything to say about it. He crouched down by Colt, staring at the stone barrier they'd hit. It was only about six inches long. They could dig around it with the opening only being a little smaller. It just had to be wide enough for them to fit through and they were good to go. This was it.

He dug until his biceps burned, but felt a pop of satisfaction when they finally punched through. He peered down into the tunnel. They'd done it. He was looking at a sharp corner that led to the entrance where they would hopefully be capturing a few terrorists. Glancing at his watch, they were a little behind schedule, but not much. They could still make it.

Colt was the first one through, then Elliot. The rest of the team followed, staying quiet. They separated into two-man teams, each one heading to their positions in the tunnel. Elliot had requested to be as close to the entrance as possible. Presumably to be on hand to be the first to grab the leaders coming through, but if he was honest, he also was hoping to be close in case Eden needed him. He'd promised her if she could get to the tunnels he would cover her and he wanted to keep that promise.

He put those thoughts aside, concentrating on avoiding

the guards and blending into the mud and dirt around him. He couldn't help anyone if he was caught and blew the mission.

They slipped into position. Elliot was about ten feet away from the tunnel entrance with a straight line of sight on anyone coming or going. Two guards stood to the right of the ladder that led upstairs, but they weren't on alert, just talking softly with each other. Hopefully it remained that way and they were oblivious to anyone about to put the drop on them.

Once he was set, hidden in a tiny dirt alcove, all he could do was wait. The dim lights of the tunnel cast strange shadows---ones that were hiding Griffin Force. Elliot didn't dare look at his watch, but he knew they had to be getting close to go time. Had Eden made it inside? Was Isaac still alive? The questions roiled through him, but the answers wouldn't come until after the mission was over.

The tunnel had been mostly silent and Elliot stiffened when he heard shuffling coming from his left. He held himself very, very still. A minute later the face of Sajid Khan appeared within two feet of him. The man that had been responsible for over a thousand deaths, including dozens of Americans, in bombings across the Middle East. That's how he'd started in the terrorism business, as a bomb-maker. But he'd quickly realized that he could use his skills to take care of his enemies or anyone else challenging him for leadership and before long, he was the undisputed leader of Jaysh al-Islam. They'd been tracking him for years and he was right there in front of Elliot, close enough to touch. He seemed nervous, his glasses slipping down his longish nose, looking left and right as he flicked the flashlight in his hand back and forth. Elliot held his breath as the arc of light came close to his position. But Khan didn't raise the light any further. Elliot was safe.

Finally, Khan seemed satisfied and he nodded to the two guards who had snapped to attention. One of them quickly moved up to the ladder and opened the door, giving two taps and a knock. It opened and Khan started up the ladder before he disappeared upstairs. Elliot was treated to four more episodes of nearly the same thing, terrorist leaders he'd spent sleepless nights and countless missions chasing coming close enough to touch. His fingers itched to just reach out and take each man one by one and put an end to their reign of terror. But he held still. He had his orders. They would have their council with Amira, then they would bag them all and finally put a large nail in the coffin of their terrorist groups.

Once the men had gone inside, Elliot settled back in to wait. They were radio silent, since the security was tight in the tunnel. But he knew his Griffin Force brothers were there and that they were going to get this done. They'd been in tight spots before and come out of it with a victory. This was going to be another one of those times. He could just feel it.

CHAPTER SEVENTEEN

Eden took a deep breath while she waited in the back room of a small medical outpost. The plan to switch her out for one of the female servants was risky, but she couldn't think of anything else on such short notice. The servants had been flown in on a private airfield and were being driven to the safehouse in a van. Luke's local contact would cause an accident and insist that the women be checked at the medical center. Luke was in the next room, monitoring the mission. So far everything was going according to plan.

She sat down on the small stool and adjusted her burqa. She hadn't put the head piece on yet and wanted to wait until the very last minute. Luke's voice was low in the next room, but she heard him sign off. Moments later, he appeared in the doorway.

"Okay, they're on their way here. One of the women has complained of a sore neck and her hand is bleeding. If we can get her alone in the exam room, we'll switch you out for her."

He looked her over. "Are you sure about this? There's still time to back out."

She scowled. "I'm Isaac's best chance, you know that. And having eyes on the inside will be invaluable in bringing Amira in." She stood. "I'm ready."

"Copy that." He glanced toward the door. "Here they come."

Eden quickly put the burqa's headpiece over her head and backed into the corner where she wouldn't be seen. This was the most tricky part of the plan---getting the woman she would be replacing isolated so they could switch places without their guards knowing. Glancing into the lobby area she counted three guards and four women. One of the women was crying and holding her hand while another woman comforted her. That could be a problem. If they knew each other well, Eden's switch would be noticed immediately. Eden sucked in a breath, hoping the potential "friend" was just being kind.

The doctor went out into the lobby to greet them and spoke with the guards. They pointed to the crying woman and Eden could see their guns slung loosely over their shoulders. If anything went wrong, there was no doubt they'd use their weapon on all of them. The meeting of the Council of Seven was too important for them to take chances. But would they allow the woman to be examined alone?

The woman was shaking as one of the guards approached her. He stared at her for a long moment, then nodded his head. The doctor escorted her to the back room.

Here we go, Eden thought, clenching and unclenching her hands.

The doctor took her past the room where Eden was hiding and she waited as the doctor treated the hand wound and spoke to the servant about a possible concussion and whiplash. The woman was quiet, only slightly nodding her downturned head as he spoke. The doctor offered her an injection for the pain and she agreed. After it was given, the doctor nodded and Luke came in, just as the woman lost consciousness without even making a sound.

Eden faced the doctor and he quickly bandaged her hand to match the one he'd just done. His kind brown eyes were clearly concerned. "Good luck," he told her, giving her a light pat on the back.

"Thanks." She straightened her shoulders as the doctor escorted her from the room. She kept her head down as she was taken to the guards. The men didn't even give her a second glance, just rushed her and the other women out of the building and into the van. Once inside, the guard in the passenger seat took a phone call. He gave the report of what had happened with the accident and one of the servants. He promised they were nearly there. Eden breathed a sigh of relief. The first part of the mission was over. She was in.

But could she stay there?

The woman seated next to her leaned over and whispered in Arabic. "Are you all right?"

Eden kept her head down and nodded. Hopefully that would be enough.

The other woman squeezed Eden's knee and leaned back in her seat. Eden leaned back, too. But there was no time to relax. The van soon stopped and the door slid open.

"Hurry, hurry," the guards said, motioning the women to get out of the van. They were hustled inside the front door that Eden had spent the better part of two days watching. She knew the building was still being monitored and briefly wondered where Elliot was. Had he already gone down to the tunnels? Was he waiting there now?

They walked down a short hall that led to the back of the house. A woman waited for them in the kitchen. The other women didn't even speak and went to separate corners and began food preparation. Eden waited until there was only one corner left and she went there. Several bowls of dough sat on the counter with empty plates next to them. She quickly took the dough out of the bowls and shaped them into the traditional pita flatbread, being as careful as she could of the bandage on her hand. The woman who had been waiting for them in the kitchen came over to check her work and after a thorough inspection of the pitas, nodded her head.

Two other women were loading up platters of food and Eden walked over to help. She needed to be on the serving crew and not stuck in the kitchen. The women didn't show any reaction to her jumping in and starting to load the platters, they just kept their heads down and did the work. Eden did the same. Once the platters were loaded, Eden picked one up. The other woman raised her eyebrows, but stepped back and let her follow the first woman out.

They walked back down the hall and went up a small, narrow staircase balancing the platters on their hip. A guard brought up the rear behind them, his AK-47 slung over his shoulder. More guards were patrolling through the hall as well. Getting Isaac out wasn't going to be easy. And she had to find him first.

They stopped in front of a door near the back of the house. The paint was peeling now, and the furniture was worn, but at some point, this must have been a well-to-do household. Eden listened as the woman in front of her murmured a password. Several that had been used in the recording ran through her head as the woman in front of her entered the room and the guard turned to her. She rattled off the numbers that had been used for room entry and held her breath. Had they changed it? Was it the right one?

The guard reached down and opened the door for her. The codes were still good! She dipped her head and moved forward, quickly glancing around the room. There was a large rectangle stone table in the middle with wooden chairs set around it. Two of them were occupied. Eden set her platter down on the opposite end of where the first platter had been placed. Taking one more glance around, she noticed a man on the floor in a small alcove furthest away from the door. His face was bruised and his clothing torn. His swollen eyes met hers and she held his gaze.

It was Isaac.

She couldn't tell if he'd recognized her. Probably not with the state he was in. Could she move closer? No, the other woman was nearly to the door and Eden had to follow. But how could she get back in here? Go get more food? She bowed her head and meekly followed the first servant. At least now she'd located Isaac. She just had to figure out a way to get him a weapon or get him out of here.

Heading back downstairs, she wondered where the entrance to the tunnels was. If she was really contemplating getting Isaac out of here, she needed that information first. They'd speculated that it was in a room just off the washroom, the building plans they'd had showing it as a small storage space, but intel wasn't exactly sure what it was currently used for. It would be a huge risk to go looking for it, but she had to. That was her only way out. And her only chance of getting any back up.

She walked slowly back to the kitchen area, trying to decide when to make her move. The door just ahead of her opened and the current leader of Hezbollah, Abdel Fadlallah, appeared in the doorway. It was shocking to see someone so high on the Most Wanted list standing right in front of her. He looked dusty and disheveled, combing back his hair as he glanced into the room behind him.

That was the room with the entrance to the tunnels. It had to be. Now she didn't have to go looking. She quickly dropped her eyes to the floor and kept walking, but Fadlallah's voice rang out from behind her. "You there. Stop."

Eden's stomach dropped, but she did as she was asked. "Yes, master?" she whispered in Arabic as she turned, keeping her head down.

He stopped right in front of her and she could see the bulge of a gun strapped underneath his kaftan. "Bring me some water. Immediately. I'll be in the conference room."

Eden gave a short bow and hurried to the kitchen. She'd been given her chance to get back to the conference room and she didn't want to waste it.

At the kitchen door, the cook and the other three women all turned to look at her. The cook approached her. "Why are you so slow? I have no time for lazy women."

Eden wasn't sure what the woman she replaced sounded like so she did her best to disguise her voice, making it a little higher and speaking softly. "Master stopped me in the hallway and asked me to bring water to the conference room. I am hurrying to obey." She dipped her head.

She could feel the cook's eyes on her and held her breath. "Be quick about it," the woman said, "then come back here and help me finish preparing the meal."

"I will." Eden turned to the sink and quickly filled up a pitcher of water. She carried it to the doorway, not meeting anyone's eyes, but keeping all her senses on alert.

It wasn't hard to find her way back to the conference room and after repeating the password again, she walked in. Four people were there now, in deep conversation. Eden slowly walked around the table, filling their cups with the water. They barely paid her any notice. They were discussing Amira and the jailbreak. Three of them seemed in awe of her, the fourth, Fadlallah, was leery.

"She's not her father," he said. "She's only a woman."

The first man, Sajid Khan, argued his case, obviously anxious to sway Fadlallah. "But she may be the woman legend talks about. The one who will unite us in the cause."

Eden moved to the far end of the table closest to where Isaac sat. She took a cup off the table and filled it, before bending down to offer it to him. He looked into her eyes and she could see the flare of recognition. He accepted the water with a murmured thanks. Eden carefully slipped her hand under her burqa and her fingers closed around the knife. Shielding them from view, she passed it to him and he quickly hid it in his shirtsleeve.

Fadlallah's loud voice sounded from directly behind her and it took all her effort not to jump. "What are you doing there?" he demanded.

She stood and he grabbed her arm. "No one gave you permission to give that man water. You do only as you are told." He threw her to the table. "I should beat you for your impertinence."

The other three men at the table laughed. "We don't have time and we need her to serve our guests," one of the other men said.

"There's always time to show a servant their place." Fadlallah rolled back his sleeve.

The door opened and Amira walked in with two other men. The rest of the council. They were all here now. In person. Adrenaline spiked in Eden's veins. An opportunity like this might not ever come again. They had to take all of them into custody.

Amira stopped at the far end of the room, her eyes narrowing with suspicion. "What is happening here?" she asked.

"Nothing to concern yourself over," Khan said, from his place at the head of the table. "Come in and sit down. We have much to discuss."

Eden slowly straightened and moved toward the door. Fadlallah was leaning down in Isaac's face. Eden couldn't look away. Should she wait? Amira was staring hard at her. She had to leave or her cover would be blown. But Fadlallah was pulling Isaac to his feet, anger coloring his low tone. Something was going down. She grabbed her own knife as Isaac was brought to the center of the room.

"Our first item of business," Fadlallah said loudly. He took out a small pistol and held it to Isaac's temple. "Should we kill him and leave his body as a message to those who hunt us?"

Eden was a few feet from the door. She needed an excuse to

stay close, to give Isaac some backup. Tripping on her burqa, she fell to the floor, the nearly empty pitcher in her arms making a terrific crash as the pieces flew apart. Murmuring her apologies, she began to pick up the pieces, holding them in her bandaged hand.

Before she could gather them all, Amira had bent to look her in the face. In one swift move she ripped off Eden's headpiece. "You have conjured up one of those who hunt us. A spy in our midst."

The room erupted. Fadlallah turned to shoot Isaac, but Isaac was ready with the knife. Eden slashed at Amira's throat, but she moved at the last millisecond and the knife made contact with her shoulder instead.

Amira backed away, holding her shoulder, blood seeping from the wound. Eden moved to the doorway motioning for Isaac. The guard was on his way in, a confused look on his face. Eden twisted his gun away from him, then turned to lay down some cover fire so Isaac could get out. Fadlallah began shooting and Eden was forced to back out of the door. Where was Isaac?

But then she saw him crawling under the table toward her. "Come on," she shouted, spraying more bullets behind him.

Isaac got up and sprinted for the door, limping badly. She put his arm around her waist and after one more volley of bullets they turned and ran.

"Thanks for coming for me," Isaac wheezed out.

She was half-dragging him to the tunnel entrance and they didn't have much time. The men were shouting for the guards, rushing to find them. But she wasn't going to leave Isaac behind. "Let's get you home."

The calm he'd been feeling fled when gunfire broke out right above Elliot's head. The entrance door was yanked open and Elliot could see two men at the opening fighting for a gun. What was happening? Both guards down below started up the ladder, but the one in the lead was shot as his head poked through the trapdoor. His body tumbled backward, taking the other guard with him to the dirt floor of the tunnel.

Elliot rushed forward and grabbed the uninjured guard. He disarmed him and ziptied his wrists, pulling him to the side of the ladder. The gunfire upstairs was getting louder, closer. They were running out of time. Elliot scrambled up the ladder, poking his head up carefully, his gun at the ready. The fight was still close, but not in that room anymore, so he crept in, trying to get his bearings as quickly as possible. Barrels and crates littered the room, with stacks of blankets. "I've breached the house," he said into his comms. "And I'm c-clearing the floor."

"Copy that. We're right behind you," Colt said.

Elliot moved forward into the hall, keeping to the shadows. The gunfire had stopped and someone was yelling. A woman. Was it Eden? Amira? He couldn't tell from here. He needed to get closer.

He moved in, carefully opening a door to a room and quickly sweeping it. It was an empty bedroom. Heading inside, he closed the door most of the way, leaving it barely cracked while he tried to listen to what was happening. The yelling had stopped and the gunfire started again.

Who was shooting? And where was Eden?

And then he heard her voice. Amira. It was like an echo of the last time he'd seen her. "Kill them. Kill them all."

He couldn't see who she was talking about from the angle he was at, but he knew he couldn't let those orders stand. He stepped out into the hall and Amira whirled around to face him. As soon as she saw his gun, she ducked behind her bodyguard. Elliot pulled the trigger and the bodyguard immediately grabbed his arm.

"Run!" the bodyguard told her, jerking his head to the right. "This way." The two disappeared down a side hall.

As soon as they were gone, Elliot could see who was about to be killed. His blood ran cold. Eden and Isaac were kneeling, ready to be executed. "Eden," he said, running toward her.

She looked up at him and briefly closed her eyes. "Elliot," she murmured. "You've got good timing."

He bent to her wrists and cut off the zipties, then leaned over and did the same for Isaac. The man looked like he was barely hanging on.

"Let's go," he urged, grabbing Isaac's arm and helping him to his feet. "Now."

He glanced back down the hall where Amira and her body-guard had disappeared. A part of him was torn. Should he go after her?

Eden could sense his hesitation. "I can get Isaac to the tunnels. Go get her."

Footsteps sounded in the hall and Elliot raised his gun.

"It's me!" Colt appeared and headed toward them. "The team has us covered for about another thirty seconds. I'll get him out of here. You two go after Amira." He handed Eden a gun and took Isaac's arm. "Let's go!"

Elliot didn't have to be told twice. Both he and Eden started down the side hall. The hallway was dark, the concrete walls crumbling in most places. Rugs covered what was left of the walls, some hanging crazily, as if the owners hadn't had time to finish putting them up. From previous experience, Elliot knew any one of those rugs could be concealing a tunnel entrance. He didn't have time to check them all.

He squinted into the darkness. "Can you see anything?" he asked Eden.

She pointed straight ahead at the same time that Elliot heard the footsteps on the floor just ahead. "She's there. On the left."

They rushed down the hall, guns at the ready. As they turned the corner, gunfire rang out and concrete bits flew into Elliot's shoulder. He winced, but returned fire.

"You hit?" Eden asked, her breaths coming fast.

"I'm okay." Amira was on the move again and they ran forward as well. But within a few seconds, they'd hit a dead end.

The hallway led to one room. The only place she could be. Eden and Elliot cautiously moved inside.

But the room was empty.

"The tunnel entrance has to be in here," Elliot said, shoving the rugs away from the walls.

Eden pulled aside the one in the far corner that revealed the broken concrete wall with a large hole in it that led to a set of stairs below ground. She stepped over it and started her descent, Elliot right behind her. They could hear footsteps getting further away and Elliot knew their window of opportunity was closing. They had to hurry. Without him saying a word, Eden instinctively knew to pick up the pace, even with the burqa making it awkward for her to run. He matched her strides. The sense of urgency was nearly palpable in the tiny tunnel that barely fit one person. The dim lights strung on the walls made for a lot of shadows, but Elliot didn't even hesitate. Amira wouldn't hide in the shadows and wait to be caught. She wanted out of here.

When they were deep in the tunnel, there was a bend that turned into a crossroads. He ground his teeth together. They could only guess which one Amira had taken.

"We'll have to split up," Eden said. "I'll take left, you take right."

His stomach clenched. They would be without backup if they split up. But what was the alternative? They had to grab Amira. Now. "Okay. But be c-careful."

She gave him a quick smile then headed down the left fork of the tunnel. He went down the right fork, the dirt floor underneath his feet hiding any noise. As he drew closer to the end of the tunnel, he could see a large rug hanging covering something. He stopped, every sense attuned to sounds or feelings that something was off. His finger twitched on his gun. Carefully using the end of the muzzle, he moved forward and nudged the hanging aside.

The bodyguard stood in the middle of a small room, his finger on a trigger connected to a suicide vest. His eyes were wide and frightened, but he looked resolved. Elliot inhaled sharply. "Take it easy," he said, his voice low and even. "*La tafeal dhalik.* Don't d-do it."

The man backed up, his finger hovering over the detonator. "You'll never find her. She'll be greater than her father." He moved toward the side of the room where Elliot could see a ladder leading to a trap door in the ceiling. Amira must have gone through there and left her bodyguard to seal her escape. Hopefully someone on the team outside saw her and picked up the trail.

"What's your n-name?" Elliot asked. The guard's eyes never left his, but he didn't answer. "Were you a follower of Atwah?" Maybe if Elliot could keep the guy talking, he could figure out how to get the detonator away from him.

"Do not speak his name." The man spat on the ground. "He is a martyr for the cause of justice."

"A martyr who died at his daughter's hand."

"You lie!" he screamed. "And you will pay."

The world seemed to slow as Elliot watched the man's thumb start to press the detonator down.

Elliot fired, hoping he hadn't waited too long. If this was his last moment on earth, he didn't want to be looking at a terrorist bodyguard. There was only one face he wanted to see and for that, he had to live.

CHAPTER NINETEEN

Eden heard the shot and her chest tightened until she could barely suck in a breath. Entering the room behind the hanging, she nearly sagged with relief to see Elliot still upright. The bodyguard was on the ground, dead, a suicide vest around his chest and the detonator mere millimeters from his hand.

"You okay?"

"That was a c-close one," he said, moving forward and gingerly picking up the detonator. "Amira escaped. Left her b-bodyguard behind to do her dirty work. As usual."

"Hopefully our perimeter held and she was picked up." She glanced over Elliot's frame, looking for any wounds, reassuring herself he was okay.

"Let's find out, shall we?" He motioned toward the ladder.

Eden poked her head up and groaned when she realized they were in a completely different spot than the previous tunnel had ended. It wasn't likely that the perimeter team had even known this was here.

"How far do you think she c-could have gotten?" Elliot asked when he straightened beside her, realizing the same thing she had. This tunnel wasn't one they'd known about or prepared for.

"She can't have gone far. You up for a jog?" She started down the alley. "She's more than likely trying to get to a place she knows well. I'd bet she's going to try and get to Atarib. It's a rebel-held town and lots of residents are sympathetic to Atwah."

Elliot fell into step beside her. "Should we wait for backup?"

"Like Colt said, we've got a window. We d-don't want it to close before we've wrapped Amira up."

Eden kept going, staying to the edge of the alley. Seeing Isaac's condition strengthened her resolve. She wanted Amira to pay, not only for Isaac, but for every person she'd hurt---and her father. Atwah had mercilessly killed innocent people, torn families apart, including her own. She wanted all of them to pay. They'd hurt the people she loved and this was her chance to stop them. She didn't feel angry, though. This wasn't about revenge. This was about making sure justice was dealt to those who deserved it.

Coming to the street, Elliot signaled he'd go left, she'd go right. Eden nodded in the affirmative. Rounding the corner, she moved past a pile of garbage, but the hairs on the back of her neck raised. She whipped around, but not in time. Amira sprang at her, a gun to her temple.

"Drop your weapon," Amira ordered. She pressed the gun into her skin. "Now. Or I will kill you and walk away."

"I didn't realize you do your own killing. Usually, you have a guard to do the dirty work."

Amira dug her nails into Eden's arm. "Shut up and do what you're told."

Eden dropped her gun just as Elliot came into view. Eden straightened her shoulders. They were a good team. They could bring Amira in, she knew it. This was their chance.

Amira pulled Eden closer against her, using her body as a shield. "Stay back."

Elliot stopped where he was, but didn't retreat. "There's nowhere for you to g-go Amira. Surrender yourself."

She chuckled as if reacting to a joke, but there was no joy in the sound. "I think I'll kill both of you and leave."

"Not likely. You may get one of us, but not both," Eden gritted out, the gun digging painfully into her skin. That was definitely going to leave a mark. She thought about elbowing her and wrestling her for the gun, but Amira's trigger finger was too close and twitchy. Eden needed a better angle before she made her move.

"Should we test that theory?" Amira pulled Eden's hair, forcing her head back until Eden's ear was near her mouth. "I wonder if I shot you right now, whether the doctor would try to help you or come after me?"

Eden wondered the same thing. He'd probably stop to help her and Amira would be in the wind. "He'd capture you first, then come back for me."

"I know you don't believe that." She flicked her gaze to Elliot. "He's a good doctor. Kept my father alive just as long I as needed him to. But he won't be able to keep you alive with a bullet through your brain." The gun muzzle twisted slightly, and painfully, into Eden's temple. "Quick and easy, though."

That wasn't a comforting thought. "I guess one more death wouldn't even signify to your conscience. If you have a conscience anymore." Even Eden could hear the bitterness in her tone.

Amira made a low sound in her throat. "Consciences are for people with no vision. You can't stop me now. I have a seat on the council, a voice in how to win this war." She leaned in close, whispering in Eden's ear like a devil on her shoulder. "You've been on the losing side, trying to stop the inevitable. And now you must reap the consequences."

Elliot moved closer and Amira immediately pushed the gun into Eden's cheek so hard that she gasped. "Stay back or she dies. Drop your gun."

Elliot didn't move, his gun trained on them. "This is your last chance to g-give up before I shoot you."

Amira laughed, her voice shrill. "You're so sure of yourself, doctor. But you're on the losing side. Still."

She barely got the words out before Elliot's gun went off. The force of the blow knocked Eden to the ground, Amira just behind her shoulder. Shaking off the stars that were dancing around the edge of her vision, she looked up at Elliot, standing over her. "El---"

She felt movement beneath her, but before she could stop her, Amira raised her gun and shot Elliot at nearly point-blank range. He fell back, his eyes wide. Eden screamed. "No!"

Grabbing her gun from the ground, she pointed it at Amira, but she was already running by the garbage and around the corner. The scenario was just as she'd planned. What should Eden do? Help Elliot or go after Amira?

She chose Elliot.

Leaning over him, she took a breath, calming herself. She needed to think critically, not emotionally. Blood seeped out underneath his body and she began to look for an entrance wound.

"It's my shoulder," Elliot panted as he slowly sat up. "I'm okay. G-go after her."

"She's long gone and shoulder wounds can be dangerous. Let's have a look." She bent over him, as he shook his head. Eden didn't give him time to say anything else. "We'll have another chance to find her. Don't worry."

Elliot scooted to the side of the building, giving them a bit more cover. He looked down at his shoulder. "Just barely m-missed the vest. I should have been expecting her to shoot. That was stupid. I j-just wanted you away from her, when I should have m-made sure the threat was n-neutralized first."

His stutter was more pronounced when he was worried or stressed. It was so endearing to her. "No one can predict what Amira will do. That's what makes her so dangerous." Eden shifted him forward. "Looks like a through and through. We need to get some pressure on it." She tore the bottom of the burqa and made a compress. "Here, hold this."

"What was she s-saying to you?" Elliot winced as he pressed the cloth to his wound.

"That you were a good doctor and if she shot me, you'd stay behind to help me and she'd escape."

Elliot's brow furrowed. "And you let her prediction c-come true?"

Eden shrugged. "Maybe it was foreordained to happen. She'd already thought the scenario through." She sat beside him. "Besides, you needed me."

He looked into her eyes, the air around them charged with their unspoken feelings. She held still, losing herself in his blue depths. For just a moment, it was as if he'd connected to her soul. She'd chosen him. He'd chosen her.

"Eden, I just . . ." he started, but footsteps sounded behind them. They quieted and both raised their guns.

She tried to shield Elliot with her body, worried that more of the Council of the Seven were coming this way. Though she wouldn't mind having her shot at bringing them in. "It's Colt and Jake," she said, as soon as they came into view. "Over here!"

Colt got to them first, his eyes taking in the scene. "What happened?"

"We trailed Amira out here, but she got the drop on us," Elliot explained. He blew out a breath. "We were so close."

"We'll have another chance. She shot him at nearly point-blank range, but thankfully it's just a shoulder wound," Eden pointed toward Elliot's bloody shoulder. "It's going to be painful for a while, though."

Colt swept the area. A breeze had picked up, swirling the garbage around their feet. "We're too exposed. We need to evac out of here. Can you walk?"

"It's my shoulder, boss, not my leg." Elliot used the concrete wall behind him to leverage himself and stand. He was a bit shaky, though, and leaned his head back.

"You've had a good amount of blood loss," Eden reminded him, putting his arm around her shoulders. "Let us help you. Take it easy."

Elliot started to straighten and tried to move away. "Thanks. I'm good, though."

Colt chuckled, and Eden shook her head and pulled closer. "I'm beginning to see the doctor isn't a very good patient," she said. "Maybe he needs a direct order."

"I'm not opposed to that," Colt told her.

"I heard that." Elliot gave in, though, and leaned a bit of his weight on her shoulders.

They all started walking back to the target area. Elliot was gritting his teeth, so Eden knew each step was painful.

"How did the rest of the op go?" Elliot asked Colt.

"Not bad. We caught Khan and we're pretty sure Fadlallah was killed. Since they use body doubles so often, we're trying to verify his identity. We're still waiting to hear on the status of the other four." Colt was keeping the pace a bit slow and Eden was glad, for Elliot's sake. His tough front was starting to slip the more he moved around and jostled his wound.

"At least that's something. Having Khan in custody and taking out Fadlallah should put a damper on Hezbollah and Jaysh al-Islam for a while." Eden wished they were celebrating Amira's capture, but the two they'd gotten were a pretty big deal on their own.

Conversation was sparse after that. They made it back to the house where the council had met. It was quieter than Eden thought it would be. They went to the command vehicle parked in the road, blocking any traffic. The monitor showed the controlled chaos inside the house, with team members going room to room, clearing the area of any explosives. More teams were in the tunnels, likely doing the same thing. Eden watched for a moment longer until another vehicle pulled up. Nate got out and after one look at them, leaned back into the car and hoisted a med kit onto his shoulder.

"Let's get you taken care of," Eden said briskly, fully expecting Elliot to argue. He didn't disappoint. "We need to get your gear off."

"I can do it," he protested, but she continued on as if he hadn't spoken.

"Gone and got yourself shot?" Nate asked with a raise of the eyebrow. "How did that happen?"

"Long story." Elliot winced as Eden helped him gingerly take off his kit and then his shirt, trying not to open the wound any more. "Maybe I'll tell you one day."

Nate chuckled. "I can see you're well taken care of. I've got work to do."

Eden was assessing the wound. She wasn't surprised to see the well-defined muscles throughout Elliot's chest and biceps. He was definitely fit. She began to clean the entrance and exit wounds, her focus on making sure he was okay. Once everything was ready, she began to close the wound, her stitches small and even.

"You could have been a plastic surgeon," he told her, watching her work.

"Not likely. I just like things tidy." She glanced over at his face. "Do you need anything for the pain?"

"No. Let's take my mind off of it, though. Tell me more about your dad." He winced and clamped his jaw shut.

She wanted to talk about her brother, to ask about that day at the embassy, but it still wasn't the right time. She looked into Elliot's eyes. "He was quick to laugh. Loved people. Very smart."

She smiled in spite of herself. "He liked to tell terrible jokes, that you couldn't help but smile at."

He tilted his head toward her. "What was your favorite one?"

That was easy. The joke he'd told her at least once a day springing to her mind. "Why couldn't the bicycle stand up by itself?"

"Why?"

"It was two tired." Eden couldn't hold back the grin. She could still hear his chuckle when he said it. Every time. Those were happy memories.

Elliot squeezed her free hand. "He sounds like a wonderful father."

"He was." She finished stitching and took out the bandage, making sure it was firmly in place. "You're going to want to baby that for a while."

"I know." He gave her a knowing look. "I've treated a few wounds in my time."

"Yes, but as we mentioned, the doctor isn't a very good patient." She handed him his t-shirt, but he made no move to put it on, just held it in his hands.

"Or maybe the doctor just doesn't have any patience." He gave her a wry smile at his little pun, then touched her shoulder and gazed into her face. "Thank you."

"You're welcome." She felt the pull between them and wanted to move closer and kiss him. Run her hands over his chest and through his hair, search for any other injuries, show herself he was just fine. But she couldn't. Not now, when so many people were around and the mission had gone sideways. Being near him, though, gave her a feeling of peace and contentment she hadn't had since her father died and she didn't want to lose that. Not again. But how could she keep that feeling?

Putting away the medical supplies, she took a deep breath. She'd made a choice today that had far-reaching consequences. Amira had escaped because Eden had chosen the man she cared about. That couldn't happen again.

But her heart said otherwise.

CHAPTER TWENTY

Elliot's pulse was still racing. He'd never had such a strong reaction to anyone before. Eden had touched something in him and he wasn't sure how to feel about it. About her. The urge to kiss her had been so strong, he wasn't sure how he'd controlled himself. She turned back to face him after finishing up with the medical supplies and he reached for her, but pulled back when Colt approached them. They both turned toward him.

"Did we get anything?" Eden asked. Her shoulders were set and she seemed more tense than she had been five minutes ago. Was she worried about Colt guessing there was something between them? Or was it the mission?

"From what intelligence we could get off one of the laptops inside, it looks like Amira not only got a seat on the council by a majority vote, but she also got approval to buy the four mid-range missiles from Kabir. Delivery by tomorrow." Colt looked between Eden and Elliot. "The meeting wasn't to interview her to be on the council, it was to discuss what they're going to do with the missiles." He wiped sweat from his brow and blew out a breath. "Also, Isaac is asking for you, Eden, and I think it's a good idea if Elliot checks on him. They worked him over pretty good."

Eden glanced at Elliot, her brow creased in concern. "Where is he?"

"At our apartment building across the street." Colt looked behind him. "He's got a long debrief ahead of him, but right now he needs a doctor and a lot of rest."

Elliot started toward the apartment at the same time Eden did, his mind going through what supplies he still had on hand.

"Hey, El," Colt said. "Can I talk to you about something real quick? Then you can catch up with Eden."

"Can it wait? I'm anxious to see Isaac and help p-patch him up."

Colt didn't budge. "I won't be long."

It wasn't an order, but Colt's insistence made Elliot curious as to what this could be about. "Okay."

"I'll see you two later then." Eden turned and walked away. Elliot thought she might look back, hoped she would for some reason, but she didn't. He inwardly sighed. He had no idea where he stood with her, or what was going on exactly, but he would dearly love to know.

He focused on Colt. "Do we know where she's buying the m-missiles? Or what they're going to be used for?" Elliot tried to lift his sore arm and see what sort of pain he was looking at. It hurt quite a bit, but was bearable. It just reminded him how close they'd been to bringing her in and this was just salt in the wound.

"We have an idea." Colt gave Elliot a once-over. "As soon as you're done with Isaac, I want you to take a break. You look like you could use some rest."

"I'm fine." He didn't want to be babied right now. He wanted to get back out there and find Amira.

Colt's eyes narrowed as he looked closer at Elliot. There was no doubt he took in the dried blood that was halfway covering his chest and arm. Elliot quickly drew his t-shirt over his head. It wasn't as bad as it looked.

"You were shot an hour ago," Colt told him. "We've got some time before we're back out there to find Amira. We think we know where the missile buy is going to be, but we're verifying some information. Until then, go back to the apartment, check on Isaac, then take a break while we finish up here. Don't make me make that an order."

He wanted to put up another protest, but knew Colt was right. He was dealing with not only the pain in his shoulder, but pretty much every other part of him ached, too. It wouldn't be so bad to rest for a little bit while they gathered what intel they could from the house. "Okay. But c-call me if anything changes."

"I will." Colt turned back to the target house and went inside. Elliot made his way to the apartment where they'd had their base and were scoping out the neighborhood before the meeting happened. Once he'd seen to Isaac and his wounds, that old ratty couch he'd seen off to the side of the living area was calling his name. It wouldn't be the most comfortable thing Elliot had ever slept on, but he couldn't wait to lie down.

He slowly climbed the stairs to the second story, wishing now he'd taken the pain medication Eden had offered him. Did he have any supplies in the apartment? He couldn't remember. Hopefully he had whatever Isaac would need.

Opening the door, he slipped inside. The living room was empty. He could hear soft murmurs coming from one of the bedrooms and he headed there. He slowly opened the door and both Isaac and Eden turned to look at him. The room was furnished with a bed, a table, a small dresser with two empty drawers hanging open, and a chair. Elliot crossed the room and stopped next to the bed. "How are you f-feeling?"

"Fine, fine." Isaac's mouth was swollen and the words came out slightly slurred. He had two black eyes and a cut on his forehead. He definitely wasn't feeling fine.

"For a spy, you're not a great liar." Elliot sat down in the chair. "Where are you hurt?"

Isaac grimaced and slowly held up his arm. "I think they broke my wrist. And maybe some ribs."

"Okay I can work with both of those. They're p-painful, but fixable." Elliot stood to get his medical bag, but Eden picked it up from the floor at her feet and handed it to him. Their fingers touched briefly and his pulse reacted. Eden's face didn't give anything away as to how she was feeling. She had the best poker face he'd ever seen.

Elliot put those thoughts aside and got to work. Stabilizing Isaac's arm, he splinted and wrapped his wrist. Eden seemed to be able to anticipate what supplies he would need and the process didn't take long. "We're going to need to g-get you out of that shirt, so I can take a look at your ribs."

Isaac nodded and slowly sat up, unable to suppress a groan. They both helped him get the shirt off and Elliot clenched his jaw when he saw Isaac's torso. Every inch of it was bruised, some in the shape of a boot. "They worked you over good."

Isaac grunted. "Didn't give them anything, though."

Elliot didn't doubt it. Isaac seemed like someone who wouldn't break even under extreme pressure. But he'd obviously paid for his silence by being severely beaten. "How did they c-capture you in the first place?"

"I got careless." Isaac's mouth tightened into a hard line as Elliot pressed along his ribcage. "Trusted the wrong people. I should have realized this was too big and the players involved too powerful for anyone to resist. Money talks."

"You've got at least two broken ribs, m-maybe more." Elliot took the stethoscope from Eden and listened to his lungs, watching the ribcage as Isaac breathed. It was obvious he was in a lot of pain. When Elliot was done, he leaned in to look Isaac in the eye. "Other than some broken bones, cuts and bruises, do you have any other injuries?"

"No." Isaac met his gaze and never wavered. Maybe he was a very good liar after all.

"Okay, well, I'm going to g-give you some pain medicine that'll help you rest." Elliot put the stethoscope in the bag and pulled out a vial and syringe. "Glad it wasn't worse for you." Physically at least. Captivity and torture would have a psychological impact. It always did.

Isaac closed his eyes and nodded. He barely flinched when Elliot administered the pain meds. The man was a warrior. Between the bruises Elliot had seen the old wounds, scars from at least three bullet wounds, a knife wound, and what looked like a burn on his side. He'd been fighting this war a lot longer than Elliot and had the injuries---both in body and spirit he was sure---to prove it.

Finishing up he moved to the door of the room. Eden did not follow, instead, she took the chair and sat by the bed. It made sense she'd want a few moments to sit with him. Elliot respected that and closed the door quietly behind him.

He set the medical bag down and immediately headed for the couch in the corner. The wood creaked beneath his weight as he gingerly lowered himself to the wooden carved couch with a pathetically thin cushion covering the seat. It felt good just to sit. He held his sore arm and closed his eyes, tipping his head against the carved back that also featured another thin cushion where his neck touched. He didn't care how lumpy it was. He'd take it, especially since his shoulder had started to throb where he'd been shot. His body was anxious for sleep, so he let himself doze off. He barely heard the bedroom door open and close.

He opened one eye and straightened, holding in a wince when he moved too fast. Eden stood outside Isaac's room watching him.

"Hey," she said, softly. "I'm glad to see you getting some rest. Sorry to disturb you."

He relaxed against the couch again. "You d-didn't think I would rest?"

She shook her head. "Not unless it was a direct order."

With a chuckle, he nodded toward the seat next to him. "You should be g-getting some rest, too. I can make room."

The only other alternative was the kitchen chair, so she came and sat by him. Copying his stance, she leaned her head back against the couch cushion. "It feels like I haven't slept in a few days."

"You haven't." She was just close enough that he could feel her body heat and yet he still wanted to be closer. "Is Isaac sleeping?"

"He is now. He fought the pain meds until after he'd scolded me for taking such a big risk to come and get him, but I was expecting that." She lifted her hand and rubbed her neck. "He's all bark and no bite."

He gave a low laugh. "I bet it took a few scoldings from him before you figured that out. You don't m-mind taking risks."

"Only when the stakes are high and there's no other way," she said slowly, the tone of her voice drowsy.

He could see out of the corner of his eye that she'd turned her head to look at him. He met her gaze. "Did you hear we got a lead on Amira?" Elliot asked, his brain starting to drift off again.

"Yeah. I'm glad we'll get another chance to grab her." She closed her eyes and let out a small sigh.

"Hopefully before she buys the m-missiles," Elliot added.

"At least now we know what she needed the money from her father's bank account for." Eden's voice was sounding farther and farther away.

"It's all coming t-together now."

And that's the last thing Elliot remembered before sleep overtook him.

When Elliot opened his eyes, it took him a moment to get his bearings. He was so comfortable it was tempting to just sleep for a little longer. He turned his head slightly to see Eden's head resting on his chest, her face open and a lot less worried. She was so beautiful. He reached over and let his thumb lightly brush over her cheek. Her skin was so soft, but the cut she'd sustained in the prison fight was an angry red slash over her cheekbone. How had someone like her gotten caught up in a war? She should have been a doctor, a partner with her father, but instead, she was fighting terrorism. *And doing a fine job at it,* he thought.

She opened her eyes and stared at him. What was she thinking? He shifted slightly, his gaze locked on hers. She didn't say anything, but lifted her chin, bringing her face just a breath away from his, her eyes fluttering shut. He kissed her and pressed closer, harder, wanting to have this moment with her away from everything else they were going to face the moment they stepped outside this room.

She seemed to feel the same urgency as she turned into him and circled her arms around his neck, a little moan escaping her. His body aches faded away as his hands ran through her hair. He explored her lips, her warmth, and lost himself in their kiss. His heart was pounding through his veins, the wonder of being in her arms something he knew he'd treasure forever. When they drew back, he breathed her in.

"Eden," he whispered.

"I know."

He'd never felt anything like this before. He didn't want to leave her side. With a quick kiss to her lips, he settled back on the couch and tucked her underneath his good arm, content to just hold her. They watched the shadows of the sunset creep across the floor as the room dimmed.

Elliot stroked her shoulder with his thumb, knowing it was time. "Your brother told us he was supposed to meet with Atwah that day. He'd been promised a position in the inner circle of his so-called freedom fighters. But Fahad intercepted him and said he needed to prove himself worthy. That's when he got his suicide vest and the assignment to go to the embassy. Ben was horrified, but thought he was in too deep. If he didn't go through with it, he was afraid they would kill him anyway." He let out a deep breath, remembering that day like it had just happened. "We told him we would protect him. He believed us. Told us he had a sister to live for. I don't know if Fahad had people watching or what happened exactly, but as soon as he tried to get the vest off, it detonated."

Tears slipped down Eden's cheeks. She couldn't hold in the shudders of grief and Elliot gripped her tightly against him. "He loved you."

"I know," she said, her voice breaking. "I always wondered how he got in so deep so fast. That answers a lot of my questions."

"I'm sorry." He kissed her forehead. "I wish that d-day had turned out differently."

"I do, too. I wish I had picked up his call that day. I don't even remember what I was doing that sent it to voicemail." She exhaled a long sigh. "I go back to the embassy in Jordan every year on the anniversary. As if I'll find the answers I need there, or just to be where he took his last breath. That's weird, I know." She gave a shaky laugh.

"That's not weird. Grief affects everyone d-differently." He leaned his head on hers. "But just know he said you were the p-person he wanted to live for. He loved you. I could feel that." Elliot would never forget the look of relief in Ben's eyes when Elliot had said they could protect him. That he had options. That's what had haunted him. For that brief, brilliant moment Ben had had hope, but that all went up in flames. Literally.

"Are you okay?" he asked softly, not wanting to rush her.

"Yeah. There's a lot to process, but thank you for being there that day. For helping him." She put her hand on his chest and pushed up to kiss him. "I can't ever thank you enough for that."

He kissed her back, lingering as long as he dared. "We probably need to go," he whispered near her ear. The invisible cord that had bound them together from the beginning now seemed to be tightly wrapped around them and he didn't mind at all. But they did have a job to do.

"Just one more minute." She nestled in, fitting as if she was made for him.

They sat there in silence, absorbing the peace of being together, both of them knowing it wouldn't last.

He didn't want to disturb the moment, knowing they'd soon be facing chaos again tracking down Amira, but his feelings for her were deeper than he'd ever thought and he wanted to tell her. "I wish . . ."

She quickly put her finger against his lips. "No wishes. We know better."

He was disappointed, but understood. Instead of arguing, he kissed her fingertips. "Okay." He'd let it go. For now. Checking his phone and not finding any messages from Colt, he knew they probably had a few more minutes before they had to go back. "Are you hungry? We should probably eat before we m-meet the others."

Moving away, she sat up slowly, glancing back at him with a smile. "Was that your stomach growling earlier? I thought it was a small earthquake from the sounds of it. I guess we'd better see what's in the kitchen."

He returned her smile. They held hands, not wanting to break their connection just yet, and walked to the other room together. Eden opened the small fridge. The sandwich fixin's from earlier were still there, so they got them out and made a sandwich. They sat close together at the table, their fingers and knees touching often, their mouths turned up into a smile, content to just be in the moment.

They lingered at the table when the sandwiches were gone, but their time was coming to an end. When everything was put away and they were getting ready to leave, Elliot pulled her to him once more. "I want so much more t-time with you."

"I know. We both want that." She looked down. "Our jobs don't allow much of a personal life."

"We can m-make it happen if we try." He lifted her chin gently, caressing her cheek with his thumb. "I want to try."

"Let's talk about it when Amira is in custody." She reached up on tiptoes and kissed him. It was meant to be a short kiss, but Elliot couldn't let it end. He moved his hands from her shoulders to the small of her back, pulling her closer, not wanting to feel desperate, but confident that they could explore whatever this was between them once the mission was over.

His kiss was slow, exploring her mouth, telling her every-thing he wanted to say, hoping she knew and could understand how much he cared for her. When they drew back, his hands trailed down her arms and he took her hand. His phone buzzed in his pocket and they moved toward the door. It was time to go. Elliot held her fingers in his until they left the apartment and then he dropped his hand to his side. The illusion was over and the mission was in front of them.

They walked downstairs and into the last of the fading sunlight. They crossed the street to the target house and their team that was gathered around Colt. He watched her walk toward David, wanting her to turn around and say she'd try, too. As if she'd heard his thoughts, she turned and gave him a brilliant smile without any words.

And that would have to be enough for now.

CHAPTER TWENTY-ONE

Eden had always been able to find calm among chaos. It had been one of her greatest assets with this job. But right now, in the car headed to the missile delivery location, her stomach was a mass of nerves. She couldn't deny her feelings for Elliot, and that it was the completely wrong time and place to acknowledge any of that, but part of her didn't care about that anymore. They worked well together and that partnership had got them to this point. From the moment she'd met him in those tunnels trying to save Atwah's life, she'd felt a connection to him that had only gotten stronger, especially knowing that he'd been there for her brother. But being with him on that couch, just being held by him, had only strengthened her feelings for him. It was as if they'd only been searching the world for each other and now that they were together, she didn't want to be apart. Though they were currently in a car, headed toward an op they hadn't had nearly enough time to plan. So much could go wrong. But this was their only chance to stop Amira from using four missiles to wreak havoc on innocent people. It had to work.

Her gaze landed on Elliot in the front passenger seat and he must have sensed her eyes on him. He looked back. "You okay?"

Eden nodded. What else could she say? They all knew the stakes if this mission went wrong. But there was an extra layer of anxiety flowing through her. She needed Elliot to come through this alive. She wanted to explore the feelings between them. After losing her family, she'd kept her heart locked away, but Elliot had gotten past all her defenses. To lose him now would be unbearable. No, they had to come through this. She wished she could go back to the apartment for one more minute and tell him she wanted to try. To kiss him one more time. Hopefully they'd still have a chance to do all of that. After Amira was in custody.

Working to push all of those feelings to the back of her mind, she concentrated on what her part in the mission was going to be. The intel they'd been able to gather had said the missile delivery would be made in a warehouse near an airstrip on the Iraqi border. Amira was prepared for any contingency and planned to have snipers all around the site, carefully hidden. Eden's assignment was to stay on the far side monitoring Amira's movements. She'd also been given authorization that if she had a shot, she should take Amira out.

With the meeting place so close to an airstrip, there was no doubt the missiles would be sold and immediately flown out of the country. No one wanted that and they were prepared to do anything they could to make sure it didn't happen. It was strange in a way though. Eden had spent months being trained and prepared to kill Atwah, Amira's father. Now she had authorization to kill Amira, his daughter. Eden hadn't seen that development coming at all, but she was ready to do whatever she had to.

Eden leaned back in her seat and took a deep breath, letting it out slowly. The darkness was starting to fade around the edges of the sky. It would be light in about two hours and they needed to be in place by then. Leaning her head against the door, she closed her eyes. Her father's face came unbidden to her mind, then her brother and mother. They'd once been a happy family with a bright future ahead of them. War and terrorism had stolen all of their dreams. Maybe today she could be part of the mission that stopped this war from escalating and a terrorist from benefitting off the suffering of families like hers. Maybe that would bring a little peace to her heart.

The car finally stopped and everyone silently exited, fanning out to their positions around the warehouse and the airstrip. The area seemed deserted, but they didn't want to take any chances. Eden flipped down her NVGs. Night vision wouldn't work for much longer, but it would come in handy for the moment. She carefully looked around. No sign of anyone. If Amira's men were supposed to be here, they were late. All seemed quiet.

She got into position on the far side of the airfield where she still had a clear view of the warehouse. There wasn't much cover beyond a few trees and a small concrete maintenance building, but it was enough. Hunkering down, she scoped out the area and caught a glimpse of Elliot as he made his way down to the warehouse, the side nearest to the small airstrip. His shoulder wound didn't seem to be bothering him, though his adrenaline was probably flowing as fast as hers was. From his position, he would be close to the action if they really did try to fly the missiles out of the country. She didn't let herself think any further than that.

After working for a few minutes to find a comfortable position in the dirt and scrub brush, she kept herself alert by watching for any movement. Nothing. After rolling through a radio check, she settled in to wait. She didn't have to wait long, though. The ground beneath her rumbled as a small convoy of three trucks entered the area. With the sky turning from shadowy to light, she used her binoculars to see if she recognized anyone.

"Four tangos in each vehicle," Colt's voice came over her earpiece. "They're heading inside."

Eden held very still as she watched the men roll open a large hangar door and walk onto the warehouse floor. Six of them looked like bodyguards and hired guns. Two were dressed in business suits. Pressing the binoculars even tighter to her face, she took a closer look. Yep, the taller one was Kabir. But where were the missiles?

Another truck approached, but it wasn't big enough to be carrying four missiles. Oddly, the occupants didn't get out right away, either. Instead, they drove to the middle of the field, closer to her position. Eden watched as the men in the warehouse looked at each other, then walked out onto the field to meet it. They approached the car carefully, the hired guns ready to fire at any provocation.

The two occupants of the new arrival sat in the truck for a minute longer. The tinted windows prevented anyone from seeing very much about what was going on inside. The doors finally opened and two individuals exited the front of the vehicle and two from the back. Eden let out a frustrated breath. The two bodyguards immediately moved to stand next to the two women who were both wearing full burqas. There was no way to tell which one was Amira.

Eden was riveted to the scene. She was too far away to hear what anyone was saying, but there was obviously some heavy negotiating going on. Both individuals in the burqas seemed to participate fully in the conversation, so there was no hint as to which one was Amira, or if either one was her. They would have to get closer or take both of them into custody. But where were the missiles? At another location?

Eden heard the plane overhead long before she saw it. It landed easily, taxiing about a hundred yards from where the negotiation was taking place. The two women and all the men standing near the truck all turned toward the plane. Once it landed, they started walking over to it as a group. What was happening? The plane wasn't big enough for all of them. The pilot got out to meet the group and they all went around to the cargo hold.

"Visual confirmation of the missiles in the back of the plane," David reported, his voice low over their comms. "All Amira has to do is get on the plane and we've lost her and the missiles."

"Do we have any c-confirmation at all that Amira is in that group?" Elliot asked.

Eden knew what that answer would be before David gave it. "Negative," he said.

"No identifying m-marks visible anywhere?"

"Negative." David's voice held a thread of frustration in it. Eden could identify with that. Those definitely weren't the words she wanted to hear. If they'd had any type of confirmation it was her, they could make a move. But until then, they were in a holding pattern. She got into position anyway, lining up her shot in case she was needed.

"We can't just sit here and do nothing. One of those women is Amira, so let's just grab both of them." David's voice was loud in her earpiece. Yes, he was a bit of a hothead sometimes, but in this instance, Eden agreed with him. Grab both the women and sort it out when they were in custody.

The two men in business suits were nodding to the women and one of them was staring at his phone. He grinned and they both bowed to the women before heading toward the car. The meeting was over and from the looks of things it had gone well.

Both women walked toward the front of the plane and Colt shouted, "Move in, move in!"

Chaos erupted as shots rang out. Eden and the team ran toward the plane. The pilot didn't even wait for the back of the plane to shut all the way before he was taxiing down the runway, leaving the women behind. Jake and Nate roared in with the car, blocking his exit. The pilot had no choice but to stop and the men got out, guns drawn. The missiles were secure.

The women, however, and their bodyguards were running flat out across the field in between Eden and the plane. Eden raised her gun and took the shot, not to kill, but to wound. It went wide, barely missing one of the women. They kept running toward a small cluster of trees, but there was nowhere to hide. They had them.

Elliot wasn't far behind them and he was catching up. "Come on," Eden whispered under her breath. "Grab them."

The sooner the women were in custody, the sooner this would all be over.

Eden watched as the bodyguards and women threw off some camouflage and pulled up three dirt bikes. In the blink of an eye the burqas were discarded and helmets put on. Motors roared to life. Eden didn't have a clear shot. Elliot wasn't close enough. They were going to get away.

One of the bodyguards was providing cover fire, but Elliot winged him as he got close. The first two bikes immediately started back toward the road with one of the women and the other bodyguard on them, but Elliot took a flying leap and caught the second woman who was the last rider. They rolled in the dirt and there was a brief struggle before Elliot was able to get up and get on the dirt bike. He roared after the first two.

Eden ran toward the car that was still blocking the runway. The pilot was outside of the plane being zip-tied by Jake. There was no danger he would escape and she needed that car. "Elliot needs backup," she said over her comms. "And we have two tangos on foot that need pickup."

"Copy," Nate said, nodding toward the car. "Go after him."

Eden got in the car and slammed the door shut. Twisting the steering wheel, she pressed the accelerator to the floor. She didn't want to lose Elliot or Amira. Squinting into the sun, she saw their shadows up ahead. They weren't far. She ate up the distance between them, trying to get close.

She maneuvered behind Elliot and he glanced at her. His face was tense, but he relaxed a bit when he saw her. He put his head down and they fanned out, one behind each dirt bike. They were approaching a village as Eden and Elliot closed in.

They needed to catch them before they got there and had innocent people they could use as leverage.

Eden pulled alongside the woman on the dirt bike and swerved toward her. The woman expertly handled the bike and pulled away. Before she could get close again the riders separated. Eden looked at Elliot and with a nod they separated, too, each going after a dirt bike.

A crowd of people was milling around in the center of the village and the woman on the dirt bike headed straight for them. Eden wanted to warn them, but there was no time. She kept her eye on the dirt bike. She couldn't lose the woman now. But the closer she got to the crowd, the harder it would be to track her. The dirt bike turned a corner and Eden sped up. By the time she got there, the bike was gone. Pounding the steering wheel, she slowly drove up and down the narrow roads, keeping her eye on every vehicle. Just as she passed the road that led directly to the marketplace, the dirt bike took off behind her, going in the opposite direction. Eden flipped around and followed. The chase was back on.

They were heading out of town, which was a relief to be away from civilians, but also a concern because there must be a plan in place. Where was their backup?

Just as they cleared the village boundaries, the bodyguard's dirt bike rumbled up next to them with Elliot right behind him. He was almost close enough to reach out and pull the guy off the bike, but he drew a gun, popping off a shot over his shoulder that barely missed when Elliot swerved away. Elliot backed off a little as the dirt bikes in front of them accelerated. The bodyguard and the woman both looked back just as Elliot and Eden approached an abandoned car at the side of the road.

Everything in Eden screamed danger and she yelled, "Watch out!"

But it was too late. The car exploded into flames. The blast blew Eden's car to the side, upending it and shattering the driver's side window. Eden took a moment, shaking her head, trying to get her bearings. Her arm was bleeding. Her head hurt. Crawling out of the car through the passenger side window, she gripped her gun. Where was Amira and her bodyguard? Where was Elliot?

It didn't take long to find them. The explosion must have been bigger than they anticipated and had sent both dirt bikes into a slide. Elliot was getting up and relief went through her. He was banged up, but alive. He limped toward the bodyguard who was bleeding from a head wound and pinned underneath his bike. The woman was lying in the road, unconscious.

Eden headed toward the woman. When she was a few steps away, the bodyguard suddenly turned and trained his gun on her. Almost simultaneously, Elliot stepped on the man's wrist and kicked the gun away before he could shoot. With swift and practiced movements, he patted the bodyguard down and took away a smaller gun and a knife. Zip-tying his hands, Elliot began the process of extricating him from the dirt bike wreckage.

Eden crouched by the unconscious woman, patting her down for weapons and also zip-tying her hands before taking off her helmet. The woman opened her eyes and Eden looked down at Amira. Atwah's daughter.

They'd caught her.

It was over.

"Don't move," Eden ordered.

The woman stared at her for a moment, her demeanor calm, considering the situation. "Do you know who I am?" she asked softly.

"A prisoner," Eden told her briskly.

Amira let out a long breath and reached out her zip-tied hands. "You've been relentless. You've caught me. I admit defeat."

Eden narrowed her eyes, but didn't respond. For someone who was admitting defeat, she didn't look defeated.

Elliot finished with the bodyguard and moved to Eden's side, swiping a hand over his face.

Amira looked up at him, her hair flattened against her head, her face dirty. "I can help you." Her eyes were intense, pleading. "I can give you something no one else can."

Elliot made a noise of disgust and squatted down next to her in the dirt. "We're not interested in your money. We have your m-missiles. You're going to prison and hopefully won't see d-daylight for a very long time." His jaw was set and his tone brooked no argument.

Amira shook her head. "No, you don't understand. I have a seat on the council. I have access to all of the men on your Most Wanted list. I can get you close."

Eden's breath stilled at her words. "What do you mean?"

"I can be your inside source to the Council of Seven." Amira pursed her lips. "I can pass information along to help you bring them down. To capture them."

Elliot looked at her, his eyes uncertain, then back at Amira. "What would you want in return?"

"To be free. To be able to disappear and start a new life

somewhere where no one knows me." Amira closed her eyes, then put her head down.

"Why should we trust anything you say? Weren't you the one holding a gun to my head telling me I didn't have your vision?" Eden clenched her hands into fists. This could all be an elaborate ruse to get them to let their guard down. Amira always had a plan.

Their comms crackled to life with Jake's voice in their ears. "You okay, El?"

Elliot touched his earpiece, adjusting it. "We're g-good."

"Be advised we are nearly to your position. Did you hit jackpot?"

"Jackpot," Elliot confirmed.

"Tell them what I have offered," Amira demanded. She coughed and made eye contact with Elliot. "Tell them."

He hesitated and looked over at Eden. What could she say? Don't trust her. She's lying? Elliot had probably thought the same things.

"Guys, we've hit a little snag and you're g-going to want to hear this one." Elliot looked down at Amira who gave him a small, triumphant smile.

She'd planned this. Eden knew it in her bones. But she wasn't going to get away with it if Eden had anything to say.

Elliot sat in the first solid wooden chair he'd found since he'd been in Syria, in the corner of a warehouse, but he wished it was a bed. He rotated his sore arm, ran a hand over his face, and closed his eyes. He'd never felt so tired or had so many cuts and bruises covering his body. They'd gotten everyone back to the warehouse, from the pilot to the bodyguards and were questioning them. Amira had been taken to a back room where Luke was waiting to question her. Once she'd gone inside, Elliot had grabbed a chair and settled in to wait. The offer she'd made to be their inside source was echoing in his head. There was no way anyone would go for that, he told himself. Amira could not be trusted. Not with so many lives on the line. No, she would be headed for a black site for a long debriefing and hopefully a cell where she couldn't hurt anyone ever again.

Weariness settled heavy in his bones. While a part of him was celebrating Amira's capture, she was just another cog in the wheel of terror in a war that had already dragged on forever. Two of the Council of Seven had gotten away besides Amira. Two of them were lookalikes who had accepted a lot of money to show up at the meeting place and didn't seem to know much about the terrorist leaders who'd hired them because of their resemblance. But the team had caught Khan and Fadlallah was dead. Those were victories, though, whenever they cut off one arm of the beast, it always grew four more. But he was determined to stay in the fight, to celebrate more days like today and do whatever he could toward safety and peace. But after this, he needed some down time to recharge. And maybe take Eden to dinner. She'd disappeared down the hall, probably to check on Isaac. They'd all had a few close calls on this mission.

The door to the back room opened and Luke stuck his head out. "I could use some help in here. Can you find Eden? I'd like both of you to hear this."

That didn't sound good. Elliot got to his feet. "I'll g-go get her." Turning, he strode down the hall. The warehouse was busy, with Griffin Force and the Chol team on the computers and coordinating the questioning of the prisoners. He didn't see Eden right away, but David caught his eye and raised his chin toward an office to his right. With a nod of acknowledgment, Elliot went to the door and knocked.

"Come in," Eden said.

He opened the door to find Eden alone, sitting at a desk with only a lamp for light. She had a photograph in her hand, one that was worn and slightly wrinkled like it had been taken in and out of a wallet several times. She watched him enter and held up the picture. "My family." He moved closer to see her with her mom, dad, and brother, standing in front of a beach. They were all smiling and looked happy.

"I'm sorry." He leaned his hip against the desk, wishing he dared take her in his arms and comfort her.

"It feels like I got a little bit of justice for them today. Atwah is dead. His daughter is in custody. I've got some answers about Ben that I needed." She slid the picture into her pocket, staring at the wall in front of her. "I would give anything for one more day with them." Her voice wobbled and Elliot couldn't just stand by anymore. He carefully reached for her and pulled her up into a hug. Her arms came around his waist and she sank into him.

"You were amazing. They would all be so p-proud of you," he murmured into her hair.

She clung to him for a second longer before drawing back enough that she could look into his face. "You weren't so bad yourself."

"Thanks." He touched the underside of her jaw. "I'm g-glad it's over and we're still in one piece."

She leaned into his hand as his fingers moved to cradle her face, her eyes never leaving his. His heartrate kicked up as he bent and touched his lips to hers, letting his hands move through her hair and down her back, pulling her closer to him. He couldn't get enough of this woman.

"Eden," he whispered as he left her lips to press a trail of kisses from her jaw to her ear. "I d-don't want to lose you just when I've found you."

"You won't," she told him as she arched in his arms, her breaths coming fast. "It's going to be complicated, but we'll make it work."

A small sigh of relief escaped him hearing those words. She wanted this as much as he did. Closing his eyes, he pressed her to him. "Luke is asking for us to b-be in on questioning Amira. There's something he w-wants us to hear."

"The only thing I want to hear is that she'll be in prison for the rest of her life." Eden looked up at him. "You don't think they'll take her offer to be an informant seriously, do you?"

"I hope not." Elliot gave her one more quick kiss on the mouth then took her hand. "Let's g-go find out."

They walked down the hall and Elliot had a prickle of unease. What if they'd decided to take Amira's offer? What did a deal like that even look like to ensure she'd keep her end of the bargain? He couldn't imagine.

With a brief knock they entered the room. Amira was sitting at a small table with a bottle of water in front of her. She was still dusty and dirty from their chase through the village. When she looked up at him, she nodded and pursed her lips. What did that mean? Had she been refusing to talk or something?

Eden and Elliot took the only other chairs in the room next to Luke. Elliot folded his arms and watched Amira. She didn't look tense or upset. She seemed resigned. Had she told Luke anything about her operation yet?

Luke glanced over at them, his face unreadable. "Amira has been very helpful."

Elliot's stomach tightened. If he was leading with that, there had definitely been a deal made. "Oh yeah? Giving up her c-contacts, telling us who the players are and where we can f-find them?"

Luke raised an eyebrow and tapped his fingers on the table.

"She told me about the offer she'd made you. To be our source on the Council of Seven."

Elliot nodded. "And like I told her, we would never c-consider that." He leaned forward in his chair and turned his gaze to Amira. "We d-don't make deals with terrorists. They aren't exactly trustworthy."

Luke flicked his gaze to Amira before he turned his attention back to Elliot. "There are some exceptions," he said quietly. "We like the idea of having such a high-level source on the inside, but need someone to watch over her. A partner of sorts to make sure both sides are keeping to the agreement."

"You can't be serious." Eden moved to the edge of her seat as if she wanted to stand, but was holding herself back. "She was buying missiles that could kill hundreds of people. She had her own father killed. She tried to kill both myself and Elliot. There is no deal in the world that would change who she is and what she's always done. She's her father's daughter. She'll betray us the first chance she gets." Eden shook her head. "Don't do this."

Luke seemed to be wavering. Amira turned her head and focused on him, but kept silent. Tilting her head slightly, she lifted her eyebrows as if asking him a question. Without a hijab and the coating of dust over her hair and face, she looked different. Less like her father.

"Do you remember?" she asked Luke quietly.

He stared at her, as if seeing her for the first time. He frowned and spoke slowly, choosing his words carefully. "That compound in Afghanistan. You were there." He let out a sharp exhale.

"Ten years ago. Your team raided our compound, but found only women and children. You guarded us while your team searched our home." Her tone had lost its edge. "In the pandemonium, you treated us well. You brought a chair and some water for my mother. I never forgot that." Amira gave him a small smile.

"It wasn't much. The search had taken longer than we expected and your mother looked so tired and scared. I didn't do much but grab her a chair from the hall and bring her a glass of water." He couldn't take his eyes off of Amira.

"What are we t-talking about here?" Elliot cut in.

"We didn't trust you that day not to hurt us," Amira went on. "But you didn't. You can trust me now. I won't do anything to hurt you. I want to help." Her voice was steady and clear and for a moment, Elliot wanted to believe her.

"You've met before?" Eden turned toward Luke.

"Yes, when a suspected al-Qaeda compound was being searched in Afghanistan." Luke sat back in his chair as if weariness was weighing him down, too. Which it probably was.

"That was years ago. And it doesn't mean we should make a d-deal with her." Elliot had worked hard to destroy Atwah's "vision" and this woman wanted to take that over from her father. They had to be objective here. "She isn't the young girl you saw then. She's a woman who is trying to t-take her father's place. The father who has killed hundreds of people. A man who is wanted internationally for his crimes. She is a part of that and wants to c-carry that forward."

Amira shook her head, little flecks of dust falling from her hair to the table with the movement. "No. I'm tired of the violence and killing. I want it to stop. The only way to do that would be to take his place and try to cripple those organizations who support and help him. If I make this deal with you, I can do that faster."

"Why have your father killed? Buy m-missiles? Break those men out of p-prison? Try so hard to kill us?" Elliot snorted and narrowed his eyes, wishing he could read her mind. "That doesn't sound like something a p-person who wants the killing to stop would do."

Amira slammed her fists on the table and leaned as far forward as she could. "You don't understand! My father was dying. It would be a miracle for a woman to be declared a leader. We are thought of as merely property. I had to show strength!" She shook her head and turned away. "You know nothing."

"So you're telling us you'll betray everything your father stood for and bring down his organization in partner with us?" Eden sat back and folded her arms. "That seems a little hard to believe with the chase you've led us on."

"I don't care what you believe," Amira snapped back. "That's what I'm offering."

"And we're going to accept, with certain precautions put in place." Luke looked around the room, his jaw set.

"Do you think giving her a handler is going to change anything?" Eden scoffed, leaning back in her chair. "She'll double-cross us and be in the wind the second she's let free."

"Not if the handler is me." Luke's voice rang with finality and his words echoed in the small room.

"You're g-going to be her handler?" Elliot's jaw dropped open.

"Actually, no, I'm going to be her partner." Luke faced

Amira. "And if she double-crosses us, I have no problem at all making sure she never sees the light of day again."

Amira didn't even flinch, just gave him a brief nod.

"It's done then. And we've got a lot of work to do." Luke reached down and took a laptop out of a black bag at his feet.

"I think you're m-making a mistake." Elliot stood, knowing there was nothing he could do. Luke had made up his mind. "But if she k-keeps her word and helps us take down the network, I'll apologize."

"I'll be waiting for my apology." Amira folded her hands on the table. "And I won't forget what I'm owed."

Elliot walked to the door, looking back at Amira's head bent close to Luke's laptop. If she was sincere, having such a highly placed inside source could bring down the entire Council of Seven and put a crater through the terrorism network they'd been fighting for nearly a decade. He'd seen too much to take her word at face value, but a part of him still had hope she'd help them. That was the part of him he didn't want to lose---the one where hope never died even in the face of the impossible. He never wanted to be cynical of every bit of light offered.

It wasn't long before Eden joined him in the hallway. "Do you really think she'll help us?"

He shrugged, then winced at the lightning-hot pain in his shoulder—from where Amira herself had shot him. She had too many sides and hidden agendas for anyone to fully trust her. "I'm not sure, but I g-guess we'll see. Do you think Luke can k-keep her in line?"

She shrugged as he had done. "Maybe. I definitely want to be part of the operation they're setting up. See it through."

"Me, too." And that would give him a chance to work with

Eden and spend more time with her. He wasn't ready to let her go. But did she feel the same?

She touched his shoulder. "How's your arm?"

"Sore, b-but I'll live." Her hand was warm even through his t-shirt and he took it in his own. "What about you?"

"I'm fine. Ready for a good night's sleep." She looked down at their hands and squeezed his fingers. "I know it's not the best time to talk about this, but it's all I can think about. Where do we go from here?"

Elliot inhaled slowly the words on the tip of his tongue. Did he dare say them? "Wherever it is, I hope it's t-together."

She frowned. "I want to. I really want to, but I'm not sure that's possible."

Warmth radiated through him at her words. She wanted to be with him, too. "You g-guys are freelancing with Isaac, right? With what happened to Isaac, m-maybe he's ready for a different role. And Griffin Force c-could use your team." The more he talked the more he liked the idea. "Join Griffin Force." Her face looked contemplative. Did she think it could work? "Talk to Isaac and David at least. See what they have to say. I think it would be a g-great fit."

She gave him a tentative smile. "And we do work well with each other."

"It's been a while since I've had a p-partner." He lifted her hand to his mouth pressing a kiss to the back of it. "Professionally and p-personally."

She reached up on her tiptoes and kissed him quickly on the lips. "I'll talk to David and Isaac. We might need to pool our resources if Amira really is going to help us. That is going to be huge."

"Definitely. And, if you're on b-board, I have a few ideas for us for when there's downtime that have nothing to do with chasing t-terrorists." He smiled and touched her hair, pushing it behind her shoulder. "I've seen how you work—you're smart and g-great under pressure. And I've seen g-glimpses of a woman I'd like to know better."

"I'd like to uncover a few of your secrets, too," she said, leaning into him.

There was movement inside the room, a scraping of chairs, and Elliot reluctantly stepped back. The door opened and Luke walked out and looked between them. He held up his hand. "I know you have objections, but I've got a gut feeling about this."

"Eden and I were just d-discussing the idea of pooling our resources and b-backing you up. You're going to need all the help you can get." Would Luke think that was a good idea?

Luke cocked an eyebrow. "You want to continue working together? I'm not surprised that's what you were discussing." He gave them a knowing smile. "We'll have to talk to Isaac, but I have to say, I enjoyed having Griffin Force and Chol on this op. We were all in sync and got the job done." He started to walk away. "I'll make a few phone calls and let you know."

Eden stepped closer as soon as he was gone. "Even he saw that we were a good team."

"As m-much as I agree with that statement, d-do you want to get some dinner and not talk about work?" He put a hand on her waist, glad they had the hallway all to themselves for the moment. "It'd be n-nice to spend time with you and not have anyone shoot at us."

"I like this plan." Her hands slid up his arms. "You are an excellent strategist."

He leaned in, her faint cinnamon scent reaching him. One of these days he was going to see if she had cinnamon candies, soap, or a perfume. Whatever it was, he liked it. "And a good d-doctor, too. Rest is always a b-big part of recovery after stressful events."

"Then I put myself in your capable hands."

"That's the best idea I've heard all d-day." He lowered his head to hers, pulling her closer, one hand moving over her back while he explored her mouth. She was a perfect fit against him, as if they'd been made for each other and had only been waiting to find the missing piece. He couldn't explain how she felt like a part of him now and he never wanted to let her go. His thumb trailed over her jaw and he inched back to rest his forehead against hers.

"We've already lived a d-dozen lifetimes in the last week, but I can't imagine d-doing this without you."

"You don't have to," she smiled, resting her hands on his chest. "Let's do this. Together."

And he kissed her again. Their line of work was dangerous and every mission put their lives on the line, so Elliot wanted to make every moment with her count.

Starting right now.

The medical tent door flapped in the breeze as Elliot finished applying the bandage to the little boy's arm. "That should take care of it. Just remember to keep the stitches c-clean while your cut heals." He stood back and gave the child a smile. "And if it turns red or starts to hurt, c-come back and see me."

The little boy looked up at him with his big brown eyes in a too-gaunt face and nodded. "I will."

"Thank you, doctor." The boy's mother stood beside her child and patted his little shoulder. "We will keep it very clean."

Eden stepped forward with two pieces of candy in her hand and held them out. "If your mother says it's all right, you can have a treat for being so brave."

He looked at his mother and she nodded. His face brightened as he took a piece of candy in each hand. "There is one for me and one for Omar."

"Your brother will be so happy if you share with him." His mother took his hand. "Thank you again Dr. Burke."

Elliot and Eden watched them leave, before Elliot started cleaning up. "He's d-definitely going to have a scar, but it could have been worse. I'm glad they're starting a school in the camp, so the kids have something to do and aren't g-getting up to mischief. I'd hate to see any more kids in here with c-cuts like that."

"He's lucky he had you to stitch him up. That was a nasty cut." Eden put away some of the bandages and supplies in the only cupboard the medical tent had. Most everything else was in boxes and other containers.

"I recall you were p-pretty handy with a needle." Elliot caught her by the waist and pulled her to him.

She laughed. "Lucky for you. Or *you* would have had a bigger scar than you already do." She put her arms around his neck, patting his shoulder where his wound was healing nicely. "Not that I would mind. Scars make you interesting."

He leaned in and nuzzled her nose. "Is that all that m-makes me interesting?"

"No. The way your mind works is interesting to me. When we were given two weeks of rest and recuperation after the mission, I was envisioning a beach or at least a hotel." She looked around her at the tiny, cramped medical tent. "I never once thought of a refugee camp."

"Are you sorry we c-came?" He pulled back to look at her. "We still have time. We c-could probably find a flight and a hotel somewhere."

Eden looked up at him and slid her hand across his stubbly jaw. "No. Being in the refugee camp was perfect. It reminded me so much of my parents and sharing this experience with you was . . . healing."

"That's what I was hoping for." He gave her a quick kiss on the lips. "I have some b-big plans for us tonight."

"Oh yeah?" She grinned and bit her lip. "We're not going to organize medical supplies again are we?"

"No, but I thought with your organization skills you would like that." He smiled and hugged her, then moved away. "This is going to be something fun. Meet me b-back here in half an hour. Wear your best c-cargo pants."

"I mean, I do have to say we probably have the best organized med tent in the region," she said, looking around at the labeled boxes on the ground. "But I admit, you have me curious here. My best cargo pants? This has to be something big."

He laughed then. "I think you're g-going to like my surprise."

She quirked a brow and lifted one shoulder. "Okay, I'll see you in half an hour then."

Elliot watched her leave the tent, then headed toward his own. Once he got inside, he gave himself a quick sponge bath and changed into some fresh clothing. Grabbing the pack near the entrance of his tent, he headed back toward the medical area.

Being here with Eden had been a salve not only for Eden's wounded spirit, but to his as well. There was just something about serving those in need that helped heal wounds that no one can see. And he'd loved getting to know her better. The past month had been unforgettable. He'd never thought he'd find a woman like her, but was so glad he had. Though from the cryptic messages he was getting from Colt, the situation with

Amira was starting to gain traction and he knew they'd be called back to help monitor her movements soon. That's why he'd spent some time planning for a romantic dinner with Eden tonight. Well, as romantic as you can be in the heat and dust of a refugee camp.

Eden was waiting for him outside the medical tent. She gave him a once-over and raised her eyebrows. "You clean up nice. This must *really* be a special occasion for you to go to all this trouble and wear your best t-shirt."

"Thanks." He looked down at his basic black t-shirt, nearly identical to the one she was wearing. "You look b-beautiful as always." He leaned in and kissed her cheek. "Are you ready?"

She nodded and they started up the small hill behind the camp. There was a low wooden table sitting near a scraggly tree at the top. Elliot took off his backpack and unzipped it, taking out a blanket. Eden helped him spread it on the ground, then he moved the table to the middle of it. Producing a small pillow, he put it to the side. "Your t-table is ready, madame."

With a laugh, Eden sat down. "So fancy."

He grinned and sat on the other side of the square table that their assistant Karam had helped him drag up the hill early this morning. "Wait until you see the f-food." He pulled the backpack closer and took out two MREs. He held one of them up. "Your favorite."

Eden's eyes sparkled with amusement. "You spoil me." She opened the MRE and took out several packages. Pushing the main dish to the side, she went for the raspberry applesauce package first. "There's just something about this applesauce."

"At least you f-found something to love." He opened his and got the heating element ready to cook his main dish of chicken and vegetables. Taking out a thermos, he poured the water into the green bag and started the MRE cooking process. It didn't take long before both meals were cooked and ready to eat. "I think this is my favorite sauce. It hides how rubbery the chicken and vegetables are."

"It's because you overcooked it." She pointed toward him with her plastic fork. "Mine isn't rubbery. It tastes great."

"Rub it in," he said, reaching for hers. "Let's t-trade then."

She held her bag away from him. "I don't think so. You cook it, you eat it."

He chuckled. "Okay, okay, you win."

The sun sank lower in the sky as they finished their meal. It didn't take long to clean up and Elliot moved the table, and sat in the middle. "I know it's not a hotel or a b-beach, but come watch the sunset with m-me."

She sat down and snuggled close. The last of the sun's rays streaked across the sky in vibrant reds and oranges, lighting up the desert landscape below them. They could hear conversations and laughter coming from the tents in the camp, little wisps of smoke from their cooking fires making the oranges in the sky that much more spectacular. Elliot's hand lazily stroked from Eden's shoulder to her elbow. It was a perfect moment.

Eden shifted in his arms. "I didn't realize how much I missed working with my parents until I came here to work with you. Helping these people who don't have a home and have just the barest of possessions has filled in the cracks of missing my parents. My family." She stopped and thought for a moment. "I'm doing what my family would have done if they'd been here. And even though these people are refugees, they've found happiness in the poorest of circumstances. It inspires me."

He wrapped his arm around her. "*You* inspire me with your quiet strength. No matter the c-crisis, you do what needs to be done. You survived the loss of your family. You help track down terrorists. Hopefully we can m-make the world safe enough that refugees can g-go home again." She leaned in and her scent of cinnamon wafted all around him. He now knew that she had little cinnamon candies that she carried with her everywhere, sweet with a bit of spice to it, just like her.

Reaching out, she put her hand on his chest. "I don't know if I can explain this well enough for you to understand." She took in a breath and faced him. "But I just want you to know that I haven't felt like I belonged anywhere since the day my brother died, but right here, right now, you feel like home to me." She pulled back just a little, her eyes uncertain.

Elliot's heart skipped a beat as her words washed over him. "Eden." She meant everything to him. His pulled her close, touching his lips to hers. He couldn't get enough of her. His fingers threaded through her hair, slowly undoing her braid until it was loose around her shoulders.

"You have my heart, Eden," he whispered softly against her lips. He kissed her again, his breath mingling with hers, his soul finally finding home. He didn't want this to end. Ever. But he drew back, still keeping her close. "D-do you hear that?"

Someone was coming up the path. "Dr. Burke!"

With a sigh, Elliot slowly stood up and reached out a hand for Eden. She smiled as they began to fold up the blanket. "We knew what we were signing up for," she told him. "Medical professionals are always on call. Especially in a refugee camp."

"A few more m-minutes alone would have been nice," he mock-grumbled. Stuffing everything back in the backpack, they started down the path to meet whoever it was. Elliot would come back for the table later.

It was Karam, their assistant who had been invaluable in helping them set up medical services for the refugee camp. Elliot picked up the pace and Eden matched his stride. "Karam," he said loudly as they approached. "Is everything all r-right?"

Karam was out of breath when he finally reached them. "I thought you would want to know right away." He glanced at Eden. "Both of you." His inhaled quickly. "The head of the Council of Seven just announced a global campaign."

Eden's brow furrowed. "When?"

"It was an online audio message from Amin Kashmiri and everyone is talking about it." Kashmiri was the leader of the al-Qaeda group in the area and one of the council that had sent a lookalike to the meeting with Amira. Any message from him wouldn't be good.

Karam wiped the sweat from his forehead. "He said they have over 200 cells of men ready to fight. They've never been stronger and the West is afraid. Now is the time to strike and strike hard. He wants all those loyal to them to kill Westerners wherever they are found." His breaths were still coming hard, whether from exertion or fear, Elliot couldn't tell.

He looked between Elliot and Eden. "He ended with the promise that there will be a battle to end all battles so everyone will see the strength of the Council of Seven."

Elliot reached for Eden's hand. This was bad. More or less a declaration of war. Their time away was over.

Eden squeezed his fingers. "Time to get back in the fight. Are you ready for this?"

Elliot smiled and pulled her knuckles to his lips and kissed them. "Do you m-mean am I ready to fight at your side? Yes."

She moved closer to his side and he reached out his arm to encircle her shoulders. "That sounds like a great plan. The Council of Seven has no idea what they're up against."

Karam dipped his chin. "You are a very formidable pair. We are lucky to have you."

Elliot couldn't agree more. He was very lucky to have Eden in his life. She was his match in every way. They had worked hard in the war on terror, but somehow taking down the Council of Seven seemed within their reach now that they were a team. "Let's go." And they started down the hill to face what was coming.

Together.

Can Luke hold Amira to her promise to help them bring down the Council of Seven?

Watch for the next book in the Griffin Force series, Danger Close, this fall!

Julie Coulter Bellon is the author of over thirty books and has won several awards including the coveted RONE award for Best Suspense and Best Audiobook, a Swoony Award for Best Military Romance and the Best of State award for her children's book. She is also a host on the popular Authors Off the Page and Book Chat with Julie podcasts.

Julie loves to travel and her favorite cities she's visited so far are probably Athens, Paris, Ottawa, and London. In her free time, she loves to read, write, teach, watch Hawaii Five-O reruns, and eat Canadian chocolate. Not necessarily in that order.

If you'd like to be the first to hear about Julie's new projects and receive a free book, you can sign up to be part of her VIP group on her website www.juliebellon.com